A
VERY
ITALIAN
CHRISTMAS

The Greatest
Italian Holiday Stories
of All Time

NEW VESSEL PRESS
NEW YORK

www.newvesselpress.com

Cover design: Liana Finck
Book design: Beth Steidle

Library of Congress Cataloging-in-Publication Data
Various
The Greatest Italian Christmas Stories of All Time / various authors.
p. cm.
ISBN 978-1-939931-62-7
Library of Congress Control Number 2018942990

I. Italy – Fiction

TABLE OF CONTENTS

A
VERY
ITALIAN
CHRISTMAS

A DREAM OF CHRISTMAS

Luigi Pirandello

For some time, I felt something, like the soft graze of a hand, over my head as it hung between my arms—a touch at once tender and protective. But my spirit was elsewhere, wandering in the distance through all the places I had seen since childhood; the impression of them still throbbed inside me, but not enough to subdue the longing to revisit, if only for a minute, life as I imagined it might have unfolded in them.

There was celebration everywhere: in every church, in every home, around the hearth, in heaven above, by the manger below; faces known and unknown dined together, rejoicing; there was chanting, the sounds of bagpipes, the cries of exultant children, quarrels over games of cards … And the roads of cities great and small, of townships, of villages in the hills or by the sea, were empty in the inhospitable night. And it seemed I was hurrying down those streets, from one house to the next, taking pleasure in the revelries of others; at each, I stopped briefly, wished them "Merry Christmas," then vanished …

I had already slipped into sleep unawares, and was dreaming. And in my dream, on those empty streets, I seemed to come upon Jesus wandering through the night, while the rest of the world, as usual, was celebrating Christmas. He walked almost furtively, pallid, withdrawn, with a hand holding his chin and his clear, sunken eyes staring intently into the void: he seemed suffused with the deepest sorrow, prey to an infinite sadness.

I turned onto the same road; but little by little, his image pulled me toward him, absorbing me, and it was as if he and I had become a single person. But my lightness disturbed me as I maundered, almost hovered, through the streets, and instinctively I stopped. Just then Jesus pulled away from me, and continued alone, still lighter than before, a feather adrift on a sigh; and I, earthbound like a swatch of black, became his shadow and trailed after him.

Then the city's roads and byways disappeared: Jesus, like a white ghost vivid with inner light, glided over a hedge of brambles stretching on endlessly, a straight line through a black expanse. Gently, he dragged me along behind him, over the brambles, and I was as long as he was tall, and the thorns pierced me all over, but didn't wound me.

From the barbs of the brambles I leapt at last onto the soft sand of a thin strip of shore; the sea was before me, and over the quivering waters, a luminous path thinned to a tiny dot against the immense arc of the horizon. Jesus took the path traced out by the moonlight, and I was behind him, like a shadowy skiff amid the flickers on the frozen waters. The light within Jesus died out: again, we were crossing the empty roads of a large city. Now and again, he stopped to call at the humblest doorways, where Christmas, from poverty and not austere devotion, offered no occasion for merriment.

"They aren't sleeping," Jesus murmured, and taken aback by hoarse words of hatred and envy uttered inside, recoiled as if in agony; and he moaned, the marks from the nails still visible on the backs of his folded hands: "For these, too, I died ..."

We went on like this, occasionally stopping, for some time, until before a church, Jesus turned to me, his shadow on the earth, and said:

"Rise, and receive me. I want to enter this church and see inside."

The church was magnificent, an immense basilica with three naves, with fine marble all over, gold gleaming in the vault, thronged with the faithful following along with the service conducted by officiants in clouds of incense on a lavishly adorned high altar. In the warm light of a hundred silver candlesticks, the gold brocades of the chasubles glinted with each movement just past the billowing of the precious lace altar cloth.

"And for them," said Jesus, dwelling within me, "it would please me to be truly born for the first time this very night."

We left the church, and Jesus, standing before me again and resting a hand on my breast, continued: "I am seeking a soul to live in again. As you see, I am dead to this world, though the world is bold enough to celebrate the day of my birth. Your soul wouldn't be too narrow for me, were it not packed with things you should cast aside. You would have of me a hundred times over all you would lose if you followed me and left behind all you falsely deem necessary for you and yours: this city, your dreams, the comforts with which, in vain, you try to lighten your foolish suffering at the world … I am seeking a soul to live in again; it could be yours, it could be anyone's, so long as his heart were pure."

"The city, Jesus?" I replied in dismay. "What of my home, and my loved ones, and my dreams?"

"You would have of me a hundred times over all you would lose," he repeated, removing his hand from my breast and looking at me firmly with those clear, sunken eyes.

"I can't, Jesus …" I said, after a moment's confusion. Ashamed and discouraged, I let my arms drop to my body.

As though the hand whose weight I felt on my bowed head at the beginning of my dream had thrown me into the hard wood of the table, I jerked awake, rubbing my numbed forehead. Here it is, Jesus, here is my torment! Here, forever, with no respite, I fret with a heavy head, morning, noon, and night.

1896

CHRISTMAS EVE

Camillo Boito

This is my poor Giorgio's manuscript: the Giorgio that I taught to read, and write, and so many other fine things. And often, as a child, he would stand on one side of me, and poor Emilia on the other, and they would smother me with kisses. I remember that one day Emilia suddenly said to me, "Maria, you have a white hair!" And she tried to pull it out. My hair was my greatest pride. Twenty years later, Giorgetta, who is now in heaven, was sitting on my lap, and she said to me in the same voice and with the same wonder as her mother, "Maria, you have a black hair!" And she pulled a face, because she liked these snow-white curls of mine.

There is nothing about my Giorgio that I do not love. But this manuscript, which I don't much understand, wrings my heart and makes me weep. I find no peace except in church, praying to God. I would have given my own good health, my life, to see those three dear children, who are no longer with me, well and happy.

SIGNOR GIORGIO'S MANUSCRIPT

I had been suffering terrible stomach pains for several days. I could not eat. I had been dining alone at the Cavour Inn that evening, and I had to leave the table after the soup. The room was cold and virtually empty. There were three Germans, sighing at every mouthful, and a Frenchman, in despair at not knowing whom to bore to death, chatted desultorily with the waiters, saying that for him there had never been any such thing as Easter, or Christmas, or New Year's Day, or any other women's foolishness or childish nonsense. Then, happy to have solemnly professed his strength and freedom of spirit, he stuck his snout into his plate.

In the street, the reddish, almost dark glow of the streetlamps could be picked out, one by one. But the very thick fog was suffused with a pale whitish glimmer, both brighter and denser around the lamps, by which it was barely possible to discern a stretch of shining wet pavement, the dim shadow of a person who bumped into you in passing, the indistinct shape of a carriage driving by, cautiously and soundlessly. Otherwise, the streets, usually so full of people and vehicles, were almost deserted: the silence seemed full of pitfalls. Everything became vast and mysterious. You lost your bearings. You suddenly found yourself at the corner of a street that you thought was still some distance ahead, or you assumed you had reached a crossing that was farther on. You sought your way through the mist, soaked through, stiff with cold, suspecting that you had turned deaf and blind.

I stumbled on the steps projecting from the church of San Francesco, and a woman's cry emerged from the thick fog. Then a ragged child came running between my legs, begging for money, and wishing me a Merry Christmas, or some such thing. I pushed him aside. I gave him nothing. He persisted. I threatened him. I was in an ugly state of mind. In the Galleria, a reeling drunkard was singing some tedious old song. Under the portico in the Piazza del Duomo, there were two police officers walking along slowly, with measured steps.

In the narrow streets beyond Piazza Mercanti, the fog, trapped between the tall houses, had thinned a little. You could see that all the shops were shut, even the inns had their doors closed. But high-spirited sounds of merriment emerged from windows here and there. Happiness reigned in every dining room. I heard the clinking of glasses, shrieks of joy, loud choruses of vulgar, shameless laughter. It was an orgy—but the blessed orgy of the family. I stopped to listen beneath one of the noisiest balconies. At first I could make out nothing at all, then gradually I managed to distinguish voices amid the great clatter of plates and glasses. A child was shouting, "Mama, another slice of panettone." Someone else was clamoring, "Papa, another drop of wine." And I could tell what the mother and father were saying, and I could just see the jovial grandfather and smiling grandmother. I pulled up the collar of my coat over my ears.

I did not know what to do. The streets were like a graveyard, the theaters were all closed; owing to the Christmas holiday there were no newspapers. I was all by myself, alone in Milan, where I had no friends, male or female, no acquaintances: alone in the world. This time a year ago, on Christmas day, after lunch in the handsome dining room of our house in Via di Po, I had been down on the carpet, with Giorgetta and her little friends making me give them horse rides, climbing on my back and using the whip. And Emilia chided me, "Really, Giorgi, shame on you: playing with children at the age of twenty-three." And she said to Giorgetta, "Leave your uncle in peace." But the children, taking no notice, continue to dance round me, and to deafen me with their cries. I then got to my feet and picked them up in my arms, one at a time, giving them the last of the sugared almonds and a kiss on the cheek.

What happiness! Such happiness!

The walk and the fog had given my body a great hunger that frightened me. The immoderate and indiscriminate amounts of pepsin that I had taken in the last few days, which had not achieved anything except to make the excruciating pains in my stomach worse than ever, were probably doing what they were supposed to all of a sudden, and stimulating gastric activity. I felt as if I could devour an ox, but unfortunately I had long grown accustomed to the dreadful tricks of the pylorus. And yet that evening I had a restless desire to have a good time. Even the grief that usually overwhelmed me completely, allowing no opportunity for boredom, gave way to yawns. For the first time in a month—since my beloved Emilia had placed her hand, already cold, on my hair, while I hid my tears in her pillow; since I had fled from Turin and gone wandering from place to place through Italy—I felt the want of some distraction, the need to talk to someone, to open my heart to a friend, a woman, or a doctor, and to tell of my moral anguish, and physical agony. A renewed selfishness grew within me. I regretted not being in Turin, where I would have dined, and chatted and wept, with kind-hearted Maria. A little before it was time to go to bed, she would have whispered to me, in that very meek voice of hers, "Signor Giorgio, for pity's sake, have a little faith. Listen: do your old nurse a kindness, say the rosary with me. Go on, be a good fellow: it won't take long. Then, you'll see, God and the Madonna will instill a great resignation into your heart, and you will gradually be filled with the peace and comfort of the just. Giorgetta and Signora Emilia are praying for you. You could get closer to them by praying a little, too, Signor Giorgio." And to see the face of that woman who is almost a mother to me smile with sublime gratification, I should probably have done as Emilia used to; I should have knelt and said the rosary responses.

I found myself near the Biblioteca Ambrosiana. Whenever I walked without knowing where I was going—and this
was something that was always happening to me—my legs
would carry me to the streets in that vicinity. In one of these
streets lived a shopgirl that I had noticed on the second day
of my brief stay in Milan. Afterward, I had gone back to
see her three or four times, virtually every evening in fact, at
about five thirty: the time of day when it is already dark and
the streetlights come on; when the to-ing and fro-ing of people hurrying home for dinner, and the coming and going of
carriages, cast a certain busy impatience even upon the quiet
stroller, thrilling his imagination.

I feel a deep shame in confessing it, but this milliner had
attracted me because of her resemblance to Emilia. My grief
was heightened by a vague sense of remorse. By seeking out
and studying—as instinct irresistibly compelled me—certain
minute and fleeting similarities between my beloved Emilia's
appearance and that of the women I met, and even the photographs that I saw, I felt I was profaning her sacred memory.
And all too often I was then forced to acknowledge that these
resemblances existed only in my imagination. The number
of times I had stood for half an hour staring in a photogra-
pher's shop window! And yet I had in my wallet four different
portraits of Emilia, as well as three of Giorgetta that could
have been three pictures of Emilia as a child. Nevertheless,
during the five days I was in Florence, I remember having
gone twice to the far end of the Corso di Porta Romana, even
though it was raining, specially to look at an attractive little
head in a picture framer's shop, in among a great many stiff
sergeants of the line and a great many ugly countrywomen
all decked in frills; a head that I had seen for the first time
when I happened to be making my way on foot to La Cer-
tosa, and which I would like to have bought, had not shame
restrained me.

The girl was always hurrying about her business, but the first time I encountered her was in front of the window of a big jeweler's shop, where she had stopped. The lights were coming on, and the gold pieces glinted, and the diamonds shone, and the pearls had a wonderful warm luster. She suddenly turned, with sparkling eyes and lips parted in a joyful smile, revealing her extremely white teeth. Then, noticing me, she shrugged her shoulders and off she went, like a streak of lightning. I had difficulty keeping up with her, but she sidestepped carriages and slipped through the crowd unperturbed, holding the skirt of her cape a little off the ground, and on and on she went, stepping briskly. At one turning I thought I had lost her, but there she was again, in the distance, passing in front of a café—and I went following after. And she turned right, and left, then suddenly disappeared.

The next day, as I waited for her in the street where I had lost sight of her, I saw her enter the doorway of a house. She was quickly swallowed up by the pitch darkness of the entrance, then came the ring of a bell, and she was gone.

This girl's smile had thrown me into a state of great turmoil. Emilia used to look at me like that when I brought her a fine present on my return from some trip. Or when, on my name-day and on certain anniversaries, she came into my bedroom early in the morning, having knocked lightly on the door and asked in that sweet voice of hers, "May I come in?" Then she rushed up to me and fastened onto my tie a pin with a magnificent pearl (the one I always wear), or put a new chain for my watch around my neck, or slipped into my pocket a leather wallet decorated with a silver pattern that she had designed. Once, no more than two and a half years ago, although I didn't want her to pull off my boots, with those delicate pink hands of hers, she had insisted, replacing them with a pair of slippers she herself had embroidered—oh, so beautifully, so beautifully. Then I clasped those two hands and kissed her brow, which was radiant with joy. Then we heard a furious knocking at the door, fit to bring the house down: it was Giorgetta, who came in with a shower of kisses, gales of laughter, a whirl of happiness.

I had no hope of seeing my shopgirl that Christmas Eve, as it was long past the usual time, and in any case she, like all other mortals, must have been busy with Christmas dinner festivities. And yet I went past the entrance to her house. It seemed to me that inside the dark doorway was a shadow. I strolled by, looked in, and glimpsed a woman's hat. The woman hurriedly hid herself. It was her. My heart was thumping. I remained uncertain for a moment whether I should continue on my way or turn back. In the end I retraced my steps, and once more, out of the corner of my eye, I saw the figure, standing there. I felt ashamed of myself, ashamed at the same time of my desire and my timidity. I went past again. I had never been able to address an unknown woman in the street, however little averse she appeared, without the greatest reluctance. And on the very rare occasions when I had done so, it was, above all else, the fear of appearing ridiculous that prompted me. But that evening my soul felt the need to unburden itself. For a month I had locked up inside me my grief, desires, and youth. I urged myself to be bold, and since the figure was standing practically on the doorstep, I greeted her.

"Good evening."

She did not reply, indeed she took a few steps back, melting into the darkness. I was delighted. I would have been sorry if the girl had been too forward. But a moment later she stuck her head out of the doorway again, giving a quick glance to left and right.

I approached her once more, and said again, "Good evening."

She responded with a none too polite shrug of her shoulders, and said, "Leave me alone. Get along with you!" And since

I made no move to go, she added, "You've no manners, and no call to be bothering an honest girl like me."

Then my pride rebelled, making me turn away, and I resolutely went some hundred yards. Ten minutes later I was back at the doorway.

Striving to make my voice sound meek and ingratiating, I murmured, "Are you waiting for someone? Perhaps I could keep you company! I'm a decent fellow, you know. And besides, you must have seen me on more than one occasion."

"Certainly I have. You spend your time following me about. Evidently you've nothing else to do."

"Nothing better, no, because I find you so attractive. What's your name?"

"It can't matter to you."

"Indeed it does. I want to know at least what name I should address my sighs to."

"Ah, you poor devil! Now, go away, at once. If my husband sees you …"

"So you're waiting for your husband?"

"Of course. He should have been here half an hour ago."

And she stamped her feet in annoyance—perhaps, too, because of the cold, since her hands, which I had fleetingly touched, were frozen.

"It's that husband of yours who has no manners. And were you supposed to be going for a walk, if I might ask?"

"A walk! You must be joking! I was supposed to be going out to dinner."

An idea occurred to me then, which I instantly seized upon, especially as I felt I had already been so gauche. "To dinner? Come and have dinner with me."

"Oh, I couldn't do that! No, no. And what if my husband were to find out?"

"He won't. We'll take a carriage and go to the Cavour Inn, we'll eat truffles and drink champagne, and have a good time."

"But I don't know you."

"After dinner, you'll see, we'll be old friends."

She smiled the smile that had seduced me and made me shiver, then, with a very determined gesture, she exclaimed, "Let's go."

The room at the Cavour Inn, where I had been staying for several days, was very warm. The flames flickered in the hearth. I ordered two candelabras to be lit, as well as the lamp that hung from the ceiling. The walls, which were golden-yellow patterned with red flowers, looked garish in that bright light.

The imperious waiter eyed the girl from head to toe with grand disdain, and began to lay the table—a small, oval table standing by the fire, which was very soon covered with all kinds of delicious things. My stomach was impatient: had it been cut open, as lambs' stomachs are in order to extract the pepsin, a rare abundance of gastric juices would have been found inside me. My appetite, my need to eat, was so great that it seemed to me impossible that I would not be able to digest. And my shopgirl had almost made me forget this treat for my stomach, a treat that I had so long yearned for in vain. She had already removed her hat, and thrown her muff on a seat and her cloak on an armchair, and she was standing in front of the mirror rearranging her hair. Holding her arms in an arc raised to her head clearly revealed the contours of her body, scantily clad in a close-fitting dress that was so light it looked like a summer dress. I sat her down beside me, without even glancing at her, and we began to swallow large oysters, and to drink good amber-colored wine that put new life into me. The old, persistent, and intolerable pains in my intestines had gone. I breathed again, I rejoiced. Oh God! At last I could eat. I had already exhausted all possible remedies many months ago—even, to my shame, those in the classified advertisement sections of the newspapers. I had consulted distinguished doctors from Berlin and Paris. And yet I had to survive on diluted broth, milk, coffee, little bits of undercooked meat. Epicurus! Epicurus! And I thought of Emperor Tiberius, who gave his poet two hundred thousand sesterces for a dialogue in which mushrooms, the warbler, the oyster, and the thrush disputed preeminence.

For my part, I would have awarded preeminence to the pheasant with truffles that my love and I ate in religious silence, quenching our thirst with sips of a superb claret. The assortment of glasses—on whose facets every candle cast a streak of brightness, like little electric sparks—kept growing in number. Stemmed, mug-shaped, large-bowled, long-necked—there were glasses of every shape and size, as well as the big stately water glass, as yet unfilled. At every shake of the table, they vibrated and tinkled, scattering thousands of white sparks on the tablecloth. The wine was like liquefied precious stones: amethysts, rubies, topazes.

Having laid out the desserts on the table and uncorked the bottles of champagne, the waiter gave us a most respectful bow that was not without malice, and left the room.

"Would you not like anything else, my dear?"

"No, thank you, sir, I'm full."

"A glass of champagne?"

"That, yes. I like it so much and I've drunk it only once in my life."

"When?"

"One evening when two gentlemen took me to dinner at the Rebecchino. There was another girl there too."

"And your husband?"

"What husband?"

"The one you were waiting for in the doorway this evening."

"Ah, I'd forgotten about him. Damn him!"

"Don't you love him?"

"Me? I met him ten days ago, and he's married. I told you I was waiting for my husband so that you, being a gentleman, sir, as I thought, wouldn't think badly of me."

"Let's drop the formality, shall we?"

"If you like."

"Tell me, have you never been in love?"

"Let me see now. Once, I think, but only for a few days. He was a man of forty, with a black mustache. He used to beat me and wanted me to get money for him. Of course, men are all the same. Here, let me tell you what happened …"

I was not listening to her anymore. I was looking at her. She was ugly. Her trim figure was not bad, but she had coarse features, a rough complexion speckled with little yellow spots, green-colored eyes, and fine parallel lines scoring her brow.

I cut in as she continued to tell me her adventures in a raucous voice, and amused herself by mixing together the various-colored wines and then swilling down the foul concoction.

"How old are you?"

"Nineteen."

And she resumed her story in a desultory fashion. She got up; she examined with curiosity the heavy gilt frames of the mirrors; she lay back in the armchairs, and on the sofa; she threw herself on the bed; she came up behind me to caress me with her rough hands; then she ate some sugared almonds, filled her pockets with them, drained a glass of champagne, and examined with curiosity, one by one, the objects on the chests of drawers and small tables.

She seized upon some pictures of Emilia, crying, "Oh, I've found her, I've found her. She's your sweetheart!"

A burning shame and anger went rushing to my head, and I leapt to my feet.

"Give me those pictures."

"Your darling, your darling."

"Give me those pictures at once," I repeated in a fury.

And she went running around the room, climbing onto the armchairs and holding the portraits up in the air, and stupidly kept on chanting, "Your darling, your darling."

Then I went into a blind rage. I chased after her, saying again and again in a strangled voice, "Give me those pictures, you wretched woman." And I snatched them from her hand, having squeezed her wrist so hard that she fell with a cry onto a high-backed chair, virtually unconscious.

I was immediately at her side with some eau de Cologne. She soon recovered, although her arm and hand still hurt a little.

Ashamed of my brutal behavior, I murmured, "Forgive me. Forgive me."

From the chest of drawers I took a watch that I had bought some days earlier, and I slipped the chain around her neck.

She carefully examined the watch, which was very small, and the chain, which was heavy, and continuing to examine them, completely appeased, she asked, "Are they gold?"

"Certainly."

She looked up, gazing into my face with her gleaming black eyes. And she smiled. In her delight, her face had taken on a new expression, with the curve of her parted, coral lips framing the pure whiteness of her perfect teeth. In face she looked like Emilia.

"Do you forgive me?" I asked her.

She came rushing over and hugged me in her arms. Then she sat down on a low stool, stretching out her legs on the carpet, and laying her head on my lap. She tipped her head back: her hair, disheveled and half loose, served her as a pillow. And seated as I was in a big armchair, I bent over to look at her, and asked her to smile broadly.

To my great astonishment the wine I had drunk and the delicacies I had eaten (I should not be able to eat and drink as much again in a year) had no adverse effect on my stomach. But they had, of course, worked upon my imagination. I was not drunk, since I can recall today in exact detail the most minute particulars of that night. But I was in a strange state of moral and physical excitement that, without diminishing my memory, robbed me of responsibility for my actions. I could have killed a man with a fruit knife, just for fun.

The girl's teeth fascinated me.

"What are you looking at me like that?"

"I was looking at your teeth."

"Do you like them?"

"What do you do to keep them so shiny?"

"I don't do anything."

They were all even, all set regularly, the upper ones a little larger and so thin they seemed transparent.

"A girlfriend of mine," she added, "the one that came with me to dinner at the Rebecchino with those two men, had a rotten tooth. You should have seen what a lovely tooth she had it replaced with. And you couldn't tell that it wasn't natural. It cost a lot, though: twenty lire! You can imagine, there are some days when I'd sell one of mine for twenty lire."

"Give me one for five hundred."

"Of course! I'd have it replaced and keep four hundred and eighty lire! Of course! Of course!" And she clapped her hands. "But now tell me," she went on, "why were you ready to practically kill me for those pictures of yours? I wasn't going to eat them, you know."

"Let's not talk about it. It's a sad story that upsets me."

She looked abashed. She yawned, stretched her arms, settled her head more comfortably on my lap, and fell asleep.

Not wanting to wake the girl, I sat still and gradually became immersed in my painful cherished memories. Giorgetta, too, had frequently settled down to sleep on my lap, while her mother read to me in her clear voice an article from the newspaper, or a chapter of a novel. But my niece's hair was as fair as a saint's halo, her face like the face of an angel, and the breath that escaped her of the very purest, purer than the mountain breeze at sunrise. Occasionally, she would stir, talking in her dream to her doll. I would wait until she was sound asleep, and then very slowly I would get up, holding one arm under her back, supporting her little legs with the other, and I would carry her on tiptoe, followed by Emilia, to her beautiful golden cradle beneath the lace canopy her mother had embroidered. It was in that very same cot, which was so pretty, that Giorgetta died, choked by diphtheria. Before she was taken to heaven, she looked at us one by one—me, her mother, and old Maria—with those darling blue eyes of hers, and could not understand why we were weeping. Even the doctor was weeping.

The rings under Emilia's eyes, which at the beginning were a delicate blue, turned to dark brown, and the soft rosiness of her cheeks changed to a pale ethereal shade of ivory. The sweetness of that gentle disposition, eager to do good, always forgetful of herself, innocent, kind, and wise, was being purified into the nature of an angel.

As the illness gradually gnawed away at her entrails, her spirit rose up to God. In the final hours, when racked with excruciating pains, she tried to conceal them from everyone with countless sublime stratagems. When I very gently raised her head and arranged her pillows more comfortably, she whispered to me in a faint voice, "I'm so sorry, Giorgio. You see how much trouble I am to you!" And she tried to squeeze my hand. And to Maria and everyone else, for however small a service, she never stopped repeating with a smile, "Thank you."

Before she died, she seemed to feel better. She called me to her side and softly said to me, "Giorgio, we were born at the same time, and have lived together twenty-four years, almost without ever being apart, and you've always been so very good to me. God bless you. But if I've ever upset you, or been rude to you, if I've not always shown the great love I have for you, forgive me." Two tears slowly fell from her eyes. "I'm sorry to die, I'm sorry for your sake. Your health is poor. You have need of a lot of loving care and"—after a long pause—"guidance." With these words she died. I sat up all night, alone, in her room, while old Maria sobbed and prayed in the room next door.

Her black eyes were open. Her black hair framed her white face; in marked contrast to that lugubrious whiteness and that funereal blackness was the pinkness of her lips, slightly parted to show the poor dead girl's teeth, which were even whiter than her brow.

A jolt to my leg roused me from my gloomy thoughts. I had a fever and my head was inflamed. I pressed the rigid blade of a fruit knife to my forehead, which was burning hot. The coolness of it felt good.

The girl reeked of the sour stench of wine. I leaned over to look at her: she was loathsome. She was sleeping with her mouth open. I then felt a sense of utter humiliation, acute remorse, and a kind of spirit of vendetta, at the same time raging and wary, stirred within my breast. I looked at the knife held in my hand, balancing it to find the point at which it would deliver its most telling blow. Then, with one finger I delicately raised the girl's upper lip and gave a sharp tap with the tip of the blade to one of those pretty front teeth. The tooth broke, and more than half of it fell out.

The drunken hussy hardly stirred. I shoved some cushions under her head and went to open the window. Freezing fog entered the room like dense smoke. There was nothing to be seen, not even the streetlights. But from the entrance to the inn came the sound of trunks being loaded onto the omnibus. I was seized with an urgent desire to leave. The servant I called told me that this omnibus was just about to depart for the station, to catch the train to Turin, but there was no time to lose. I put a five hundred-lire note into a sealed envelope, which I handed the servant, saying, "Give this letter to the lady when she wakes, and send her home in a carriage. Then pack my bags with all that you find on the tables and in the drawers. Here are the keys. Send everything to my address in Turin. But first post me the bill, which I haven't time to wait for now."

I threw my coat over my shoulders and left.

These papers were entrusted to me by Signor Giorgio three days after he arrived back in Turin. He had returned from Milan all but cured of his serious stomach ailment, and more active, more lively than before. I felt relieved. He wrote for a good part of the day, and when I asked him, "What is it that you're writing so furiously, Signor Giorgio?" he replied, "I'm writing my ugly confessions and doing my penance." Then he added in a most sad and resigned tone of voice, "My dear Maria, it's a terrible penance!"

On the morning of the fourth day he was unable to get out of bed. He had a burning fever. After a long visit the doctor shook his head and as he left he said in my ear, "This is the end."

Signor Giorgio could not swallow anything, not even diluted milk. And his fever continued more violently than ever. He was so weak, he could hardly lift his arm. He raved almost the whole time. He talked to himself under his breath. I often heard the names of Giorgetta and Signora Emilia, and at such moments his face would take on a blissful expression, bliss that reduced me to tears. Then his face would darken again, and he would close his eyes, as though some fearful image was tormenting him.

One evening, the seventh after Signor Giorgio's return, a servant came to fetch me. My patient seemed to be asleep, and I dared to leave him alone just for a moment. There was a woman wanting to speak to him. She insisted, she shouted. What a woman! How vulgar she looked! How brazen in her speech and manners! Never had such a woman set foot in this house before. She claimed that Signor Giorgio owed her money, how much I don't know, and that she had come from Milan specially to collect it. I tried to quiet her, and just so that she would go I promised to let her in the following morning.

She seemed prepared to leave, but as I returned to the bedroom she quietly followed behind me, and Signor Giorgio, who had woken up, saw her. I put my hands together and begged her not to move and not to speak.

In the pale glow of the night lamp, my poor sick Giorgio stared at that despicable woman. His face grew serene, and he beckoned her close with his hand. "Emilia!" he murmured. It was a sweet delirium, and certainly full of many fond images that could be seen on the dying man's face. He wanted to say something, but he kept repeating certain words in such a faint voice that even I could not understand him. At last I managed to grasp that he was asking for the pearl necklace—a magnificent thing, his last present to Emilia, given to her a few days before she died. I took it from the cabinet and handed it to him.

He accepted it with both hands. And making an effort I would not have thought him capable of, and indicating to that dreadful woman to bend down, he very slowly placed it around her neck. He smiled with sublime tranquility.

Having avidly examined the precious necklace, the woman twisted her lips in a smile of such base joy that it was a horror to see. A black gap, right in the middle of those white teeth, made her look even more sinister. Signor Giorgio stared at her, screamed with fright, then turned away, burying his face in the bolster, and breathed his last.

1873

CANITUCCIA

Matilde Serao

Sitting on the wooden bench in the shadows beneath the hearth's broad black hood, Pasqualina recited the rosary with her hands under her apron. Only the *psss psss* of her moving lips could be heard as she murmured her prayers. Night was falling and there was no light left in the smoke-blackened kitchen, with its great greenish-brown wooden table, dark cupboard, and chairs with painted backs. The hearth fire, half-extinguished, lay hidden beneath the cinders.

A wooden clog banged against the closed door. Pasqualina got up and opened the door, and Teresa, also known as "Cloth-head" because she had worked as a maid for the nuns in a convent in Sessa, came in with the water bucket on her head, stooped over a bit because she was tall, thin, and bony. Pasqualina helped her to put the bucket down on the floor. Teresa stood motionless for a moment, without breathing hard in spite of the great weight she had borne. Then she unwound the rag she had used to support the bucket on her head and spread it over a chair because it was soaking wet, as were both the cotton handkerchief she wore knotted around her head and her tousled gray locks.

In the meantime Pasqualina had lit one of those brass oil lamps with three beaks and a wick made of cotton wool that soaks in the oil, while holding up—hanging on thin brass chains—the snuffer, wick trimmer, and poker. Then she opened the wooden cupboard and cut a long, thick piece of stale brown bread, added to it a small piece of strong *cacio* cheese, and gave Teresa her supper.

"And Canituccia?" Pasqualina asked.

"I haven't seen her."

"It's late and that little smart-ass isn't back yet."

"She'll come."

"Tere', remember that tomorrow afternoon at one o'clock you have to go to Carinola to carry that sack of corn."

"Yes'm."

Without eating, Teresa stuck the bread and cheese in the deep pocket of her apron. She stayed a little while longer, with her mouth half-open and her whole face dazed and devoid of expression, not displaying the least sign of weariness.

"I'm going. Good night to you, ma'am."

"Good night."

And slowly Teresa went off toward Via della Croce, where four young-sters were waiting for her in a little room for their supper.

Pasqualina stood on the threshold and called:

"Canituccia!"

No one answered. Evening had come on this February day. Pasqualina struggled to see in the darkness. She called out again loud and long:

"Canituccia, Canituccia!"

Mumbling curses, Pasqualina then went down the narrow walkway that, bisecting the vegetable garden, led from the door of the house to the front gate. From there she looked toward the Carinola road, toward the road lead-ing from the crossroads to the church of the Blessed Virgin, and toward the single street cutting in two the little village of Ventaroli.

"She must have dropped dead, that lousy girl," Pasqualina muttered.

In reply, she heard a low lament. Canituccia was sitting on the step to the front gate, hunched over, with her head almost between her knees, and her hands in her hair, moaning.

"Ah, so you're here, and you don't answer me when I call? May you hang for that! What? Why are you crying? Did they give you a thrashing? And where is Ciccotto?"

Canituccia, who was seven years old, didn't answer, but moaned more loudly.

"Why did you come back so late? And Ciccotto? Tell the truth: Did you lose Ciccotto?"

The old peasant spinster's angry voice grew frightening.

Canituccia threw herself sobbing onto the ground face down, with her arms outspread.

She had lost Ciccotto.

"Ah, you scamp, you murderer of what's mine, you're nothing but the daughter of a whore! You lost Ciccotto? Take this. You lost Ciccotto? Take that. You lost Ciccotto? Here's some more."

Pasqualina punched, kicked, and slapped the little girl. Canituccia struggled to try to shield herself from the blows, shrieking without crying. When Pasqualina grew tired, she gave the child a shove and said in a hoarse voice:

"Listen, smart-ass, I only let you live with me out of charity. If you don't leave now and go look for Ciccotto in the countryside, and if you don't bring him back home, remember that I'll make you die on the street like the daughter of a bitch that you are."

Canituccia, who was still shrieking from the beating she'd just been given, hoisted her ragged skirt—made out of red cloth—and set off barefoot toward the road for the church of the Blessed Virgin. As she walked, she looked to her left and right in the hedges and in the farmers' fields, calling to Ciccotto in a low voice. She had lost him on the way home: she hadn't realized that he wasn't following her any longer. But in the dark of night she couldn't see anything. Canituccia walked on mechanically, stopping every so often to look around without being able to see. Her bare feet, which had turned a deep burgundy red in color from a whole winter's worth of cold, no longer felt either the ground beneath them, which was growing icy cold, or the stones over which she stumbled. She was not afraid of the night or the lonely countryside: she just wanted to get Ciccotto back. All she could hear were Pasqualina's threats not to feed her if she didn't bring him home. She felt a gnawing, intense hunger that was twisting her stomach into knots. If she brought Ciccotto back, she'd eat: this was her one and only thought. So she called and called to him, walking fast between the tall hedges, a tiny speck of motion in that nocturnal calm:

"Here, Ciccotto! My darling Ciccotto, where are you? Come to your Canituccia! Ciccotto, Ciccotto, Ciccotto, come to Canituccia! If I don't bring you home, Mama Pasqualina won't give me anything to eat. O Ciccotto, o Ciccotto!"

She came out onto the main road that leads to Cascano, to Serra, and to Sparanisi. In the gloom of night the road shone white, and the desolate child's little shadow cast strange, distorted figures on the ground. Her voice grew weary. She began to run wildly now, calling to Ciccotto with all her might. Twice she sat down on the ground, defeated and in despair: and twice she got up and started to run again. Finally, in Antonio Jannotta's field, she heard something like a small grunt, then something like a little gallop, and Ciccotto came to brush up against her feet with his snout.

Ciccotto was a pinkish-white piglet, rather chubby and round, with a gray spot on his back. Canituccia shouted with joy, took Ciccotto in her arms, and started back with the last strength left in her young legs. Laughing and talking, she hugged Ciccotto to her chest to keep him from escaping, while the piglet, with his short legs dangling in the air, grunted contentedly. Canituccia started to run, thinking that she'd once again be able to eat. From afar she spotted Pasqualina's figure at the gate, and when within earshot Canituccia shouted to her:

"I found Ciccotto, I found my darling Ciccotto."

She soon reached Pasqualina and triumphantly handed the piglet over to her. In the darkness, Pasqualina grinned. They went back into the house and Ciccotto was put into his pen, where he ate and immediately fell asleep. Breathing heavily, Canituccia watched everything that Pasqualina did. The little girl too was hungry, like Ciccotto; she followed Pasqualina into the kitchen, looking at her with big wild eyes that were unable to ask. Then Canituccia sat down on the raised edge of the hearth, without saying a thing. The peasant woman had taken her place on the bench and returned to her rosary, praying in a passionless monotone. Canituccia, doubled over in order not to feel the spasms in her stomach, followed the prayer with her eyes. She was no longer able to think at all: she was just hungry. Only a half hour later, when she had finished reciting the *Salve Regina*, did Pasqualina get up, open the cupboard, cut a piece of bread, put a few cold leftover beans on a little plate, and give Canituccia her supper. Still seated on the raised edge of the hearth, the girl ate hungrily. She had a small head, with a tiny white face full of freckles and frizzy hair that was a little bit reddish and a little bit yellowish, with some dirty chestnut brown mixed in for good measure. Her head was in fact too small, and set atop a scrawny body. She wore a white cotton shirt that was all patches, a waistcoat made of brown lightweight canvas, and a piece of red cloth as her skirt, held up at the waist by a short strand of rope. Her skinny legs showed, as did her bare, thin neck whose tendons looked like taut cords. Canituccia ate with a spoon made of blackened wood, and afterward went to drink from the bucket.

The peasant woman had taken up her distaff and was spinning.

"Get to bed now," Pasqualina said to the girl.

Canituccia opened the door of the pantry, where the apples were kept. She threw off her red skirt, lay down on some wretched straw bedding, pulled a rag made from an old yellow bedcover over her feet, and fell asleep. As she sat there spinning, Pasqualina thought about Canituccia with a certain diffidence. Her little servant was the illegitimate offspring of Maria the Redhead, as she was known. With her flaming hair and carnation-red lips, Maria had first sinned with the cobbler Giambattista. But he had gone off to become a soldier, and Maria had become the lover of Gasparre Rossi, a local gentleman. Then he too deserted Maria, although it was said that Candida—nicknamed Canituccia— was his daughter. There was no doubt that Maria, after a month at Sessa, had left Canituccia and gone off, some said to Capua while others said to Naples, to work as a prostitute. Gasparre hadn't wanted to take care of the abandoned child, so she grew up in the household of Pasqualina and Crescenzo Zampa, who were sister and brother. But the girl's white face, all dotted with freckles, reminded Pasqualina of Maria the Redhead. Pasqualina—a thin and virginal spinster with bony red hands, yellow teeth, and coal-black eyes, who had never married because her brother had refused to give her a dowry—trembled with hysterical terror at the thought of Maria the Redhead's amorous follies, and didn't trust her little bastard child. So the next day, fearful that Canituccia would lose Ciccotto again, Pasqualina tied one end of a rope to the piglet's foot, and the other end around the girl's waist, in order to keep them together. Following Canituccia, Ciccotto leapt about in his haste to get to pasture. They spent the day together in the field, looking for the first spring grasses and weeds. Many times Canituccia coaxed Ciccotto to a spot where she'd seen grass growing that he might like; sometimes Ciccotto dragged Canituccia toward a green field. At noon the girl ate a piece of bread. They wandered together through the spring afternoon until dusk fell, and separated only when back at home, where Ciccotto went right to sleep and Canituccia, after having gulped down cold chicory soup, or a few chickpeas, or a bit of pork rind with bread, also retired for the night. Pasqualina was surely no greedier or fiercer than other peasant women, but she herself was not so well off and ate only a bit of meat on Sundays. Sometimes she beat Canituccia, but no more often than the other peasant women beat their own children.

Later on, in summer, Canituccia and Ciccotto were together for longer stretches of time. They left at dawn to search for corncobs, figs, and the first windfall apples, and Ciccotto had grown big and strong, while Canituccia was still skinny and weak. Sometimes Ciccotto ran too fast for the girl, and she felt herself being dragged along behind him over the cracked dry ground, worn out beneath the burning summer sun.

"Wait, Ciccotto, wait for me, my dearest!" she would say, exhausted.

Then Ciccotto would go to sleep and the girl would lie, with her eyes closed, on the ground along the furrows where the wheat had been harvested, sensing the blazing sun beneath her eyelids. She would get back up on her feet again, dazed, her cheeks red and her tongue swollen. By now there was no longer any need for the rope, because Ciccotto had become obedient. Canituccia had gotten a long stick with which to herd the pig and keep him from ending up under the wheels of the carts going along the main road. They would head back home in the evening, with Ciccotto coming along slowly and Canituccia a little ahead of him, driven by the insatiable hunger gnawing at her stomach. Once they tried to steal some sorbs in Nicola Passaretti's field, but the sorbs were terribly bitter and Nicola thrashed her like a little thief. Even worse, Nicola told Pasqualina Zampa about it, and she too beat Canituccia. The girl went off through the fields with Ciccotto, weeping and saying to him:

"Pasqualina beat me because I'm a thief."

But Ciccotto shook his head and began to graze. Still, every so often, when an idea appeared in Canituccia's closed-off mind, she spoke about it to Ciccotto. When they were heading home, she told him:

"Let's go home now, and Ciccotto will go to his pen and Mama Pasqualina will feed him dinner, and then she'll give Canituccia some soup, and I'll eat it all."

And in the morning:

"If Ciccotto doesn't run, and if he always stays near Canituccia, then Canituccia will take him up the mountainside to our parish priest Don Ottaviano's little tree, where she will get him lots and lots of apples to eat, while Canituccia eats some bread."

When autumn came, Ciccotto had become quite fat and hefty. Once he knocked the girl down with a blow of his head, but she got up, moved away from him, and showered him with stones. But that was the only time they quarreled. Canituccia ate less and less, and Pasqualina was sharper and sharper with the daughter of Maria the Redhead, for the harvest had been poor and the chaste old maid had a terrible suspicion that her brother, Crescenzo, had begun an affair with Rosella from Nocelleto: two *caciocavallo* cheeses and a ham had vanished from the pantry, and then Crescenzo had bought a gold ring for three lire at the market in Sessa. At home, Pasqualina became increasingly angry and stingy. She was always yelling at her maid, Teresa, at the gardener, Giacomo, at Canituccia, and at everyone else. On the last Sunday of the month, Don Ottaviano didn't want to give her communion because of the many sins she'd committed in her thoughts.

Then it didn't stop raining, and every day Ciccotto and Canituccia came home soaking wet. The girl put her bit of red cloth on her head, but then she had only her shirt around her legs, and as she walked through puddles of water and mud, lashed by rain, she would say to Ciccotto:

"Let's run, Ciccotto my darling, let's run because it's raining and I'm wet all over; let's run because at home there's a fire going and we can warm ourselves."

But often the fire was out, and Canituccia had to go off to sleep still soaking wet from the rain. That November, people in Ventaroli said that Maria the Redhead had died of typhoid fever in Capua and, after Mass, the parish priest used her fate as an example in his sermon, which made both Concetta, daughter of Raffaele Palmese, and Nicoletta, daughter of Peppino Morra, blush because they had some remorse on their conscience. Canituccia was told that her mother was dead, but the child didn't seem to grasp what was being said, as if she were deaf and dumb.

In that same month of November, Ciccotto had become so big and so fat that he could no longer be taken to graze far from home: he had to use sober, deliberate steps to walk now. Canituccia called to him, but in vain: he no longer had enough strength to come. The first time that she left him at home to go for firewood in the mountains, she gathered a heap of acorns in the woods, tied them up in a rag, and brought them to him.

She went to check on Ciccotto before going out to run to the water fountain, or out to the fields to bring food to Crescenzo, or to do other errands. Upon her return, before entering the kitchen she would go to greet him again. It scared the girl a little to see him so big—and so much bigger than she was, for she was as thin as a broomstick.

One December evening, when Canituccia came back from the water fountain, she found the parish priest, Don Ottavio, engaged in a lively discussion with Nicola Passaretti and Crescenzo: the three of them then went to have a look at Ciccotto before returning to their conversation. Canituccia did not understand. The next evening, however, the butcher, Sabatino Carinola, came to the house, as did Gasparre Rossi's servant Rosaria, to give Teresa a hand. There was great commotion in the courtyard and in the kitchen. A large cauldron had been placed over a roaring fire on the hearth. All the biggest platters, all the basins, and all the buckets were ready: the scales were set up in one corner: knives, cleavers, and funnels were laid out on the kitchen table. Pasqualina, Teresa, and Rosaria had put on shorter skirts and white aprons. Sabatino came and went with an air of self-importance. Canituccia saw everything but understood nothing.

In a low voice she asked Teresa:

"What are we doing tonight?"

"Christmas has come, Canitù. We're going to kill and butcher Ciccotto."

Although feeling somewhat shaky on her feet, Canituccia then went to squat in a corner of the courtyard to watch Ciccotto be killed. In the flickering light she saw them drag him into the courtyard, with Nicola Passaretti and Crescenzo holding him. She heard the pig's desperate squeals, because he didn't want to die, and she saw Sabatino's knife cut Ciccotto's throat. She watched them cut the pig's head off by slicing through the neck all the way around, before laying it on a platter on a bed of fresh laurel leaves. Then she saw his body cut in half before the halves were weighed with the scales; she heard their cries of joy when the weight was announced—over three hundred pounds. She didn't move from that dark corner of the courtyard. Time passed: it was a freezing cold December night. They called her into the kitchen. Rosaria and Teresa were using small funnels to force sausage meat into the pig's intestines. Sabatino and Crescenzo were dealing with the hams and the bigger hunks of lard, while Nicola was watching over the cauldron, in which little white bits of lard were melting down, to become cracklings and pork fat. In one corner of the hearth, Pasqualina was frying the pig's blood in a pan over the fire. Everyone was chattering loudly and gaily, caught up in the joy of all that meat and all that fat and all that prosperity, and inflamed by the heat of the fire and the work. Canituccia held back at the threshold, watching, but without entering the kitchen.

Pasqualina, thinking that the child hadn't eaten all day and that it was a festive occasion, took a piece of black bread and put a little bit of fried blood on it, before saying to Canituccia:

"Eat this."

But the little girl said no by simply shaking her head, even though she was dying of hunger.

1902

FAMILY INTERIOR

Anna Maria Ortese

Anastasia Finizio, the older daughter of Angelina Finizio and the late Ernesto, one of Chiaia's leading hairdressers, who only a few years earlier had retired to a sunny and tranquil enclosure in the cemetery of Poggioreale, had just returned from High Mass (it was Christmas Day) at Santa Maria degli Angeli, in Monte di Dio, and still hadn't made up her mind to take off her hat. Tall and thin, like all the Finizios, with the same meticulous, glittering elegance, which contrasted sharply with the dullness and indefinable decrepitude of their horsey figures, Anastasia paced up and down the bedroom she shared with her sister, Anna, unable to contain a visible agitation. Only a few minutes earlier, everything had been indifference and peace, coldness and resignation in her heart of a woman on the verge of forty, who, almost without realizing it, had lost every hope of personal happiness and adapted fairly easily to a man's life—all responsibility, accounts, work. In the same place where her father had styled the most demanding heads of Naples, she had a knitwear shop, and with that she supported the household: mother, aunt, sister, two brothers, one of whom was about to get married. Apart from the pleasure of dressing like a sophisticated woman of the big city, she didn't know or wish for anything else. And now in an instant, she was no longer herself. Not that she was ill, not at all, but she felt a happiness that wasn't really happiness so much as a revival of the imagination she had believed dead, a disorientation. The fact that she had reached an excellent position in life, that she dressed well, and the many moral satisfactions she gained from maintaining all those people— these had disappeared, or almost, like a whirlwind, confronted by the hope of being young and a woman again. In her brain, at that moment, there was true confusion, as if an entire crowd were shouting and lamenting, pleading for mercy, before someone who had come to announce, in an equivocal way, something extraordinary. She was still stunned by the bellowing of the organ, by the furor of the hymns, dazzled by the sparkle of gold and silver on the reds and whites of the sacred vestments, by the twinkling lights; her head was still heavy with the penetrating scent of lilies and roses, mixed with the funereal odor of incense, when, upon reaching the entrance, and stretching out her arms toward the plain, everyday air, she had run into Lina Stassano, the sister of her future sister-in-law, and thus learned that, after years of absence, a certain Antonio Laurano, a youth she had once considered, was back in Naples. "His health isn't bad, but he says he's tired of being at sea, and wants to find a job in Naples. He said to me: If you see Anastasia Finizio give her a special greeting." That was all; it could be much, or nothing, but this time—as if something had broken in her rigid mental mechanism, the old control, all the defenses of a race forced to greater and greater sacrifices because there would be hell to pay if they weren't made—Anastasia, who had always been so cold and cautious, let herself go, as if bewitched, into the digressions of a feeling as obscure as it was extraordinary.

"Ah, Madonna!" she was saying in her mind, without being aware herself of this mysterious conversation she was having. "If it were true! If Lina Stassano isn't wrong ... if that really is Antonio's feeling for me! But why couldn't it be? What's odd about it? I'm not bad-looking ... and I can't even say I'm old, although twenty years have gone by. I have no illusions; I look at reality, I do look. I'm independent ... I have a position ... money ... He's tired of sailing ... maybe disappointed ... he wants to settle in Naples ... I could help him ... Perhaps he needs security, affection ... he's not looking for a girl

but a woman. And I, on the other hand, what sort of life do I lead? House and shop, shop and house. I'm not like my sister, Anna, who still wears her hair down and plays the piano. The young men, now, no longer notice me, and if I didn't dress well and use an expensive perfume, they wouldn't even bother to say hello. I'm not old yet, but I'm about to get old. I didn't realize it, but it's so. Either Antonio really does have feelings for me, loves me, and needs me, or I'm lost. I'll always have my clothes, of course, but even the statues in church have clothes, and the people in photographs have clothes."

She'd never spoken this way before; her language tended toward comments about income and outflow, or, at most, interesting observations about this year's fashions. Therefore she was astonished and discouraged, like someone who for the first time sees a wretched and silent town, and is told that she has been living there, thinking that she has been seeing palaces and gardens where there was only gravel and nettles; and Anastasia, considering in a flash that her life had been nothing but servitude and sleep, and was now about to decline, stopped walking and looked around her with an air of bewilderment.

The window of the room, which was large and clean, but sparsely furnished, with two iron bedsteads, a wardrobe, and some chairs set here and there on the redbrick floor, and above the beds and the wardrobe an olive branch from the previous Easter—that window was open, and from outside a deep blue light entered, intense and at the same time cold, as if the sky from which it came were completely new to this earth, without the old intimate warmth of long ago. Not a cloud could be seen, not the smallest spot, or even the sun, and that fragment of walls and cornices that appeared at the level of the windowsill—faded, ethereal, like a drawing—seemed the world's dribbles rather than its reality. Not a voice or a cry could be heard from the inhabitants of Naples, and in that moment Anastasia, standing near the window, her brow slightly furrowed, her heart heavy—whether with hope or anguish she no longer knew—looked down, almost not recognizing the places or the people. It seemed to her that the upward-sloping street, three stories below her, had a mysterious depth and sadness. The pavement, still dark from the night's rain, was strewn with all the wood shavings and refuse from Christmas Eve. Many people were going to Mass or returning, and, meeting, stopped for a moment to exchange good wishes, a greeting, but one had to pay attention to distinguish the voices ("Merry Christmas!" "Good wishes to you and all your family!" "Same to you!"). Thanks to the beauty of the day, windows were open as far as the eye could see, and here and there one could glimpse a narrow black iron headboard, the white coverlet of a bed, the gilded oval frame of a dark painting, a chandelier's glittering branch, the brown wallpaper with a design of gilded columns in a living room. There was plenty of activity going on in the kitchens, but the men were all free, some shaving, some collapsed, inert, against a windowsill, some staring out across the red flowerpots on a balcony. One, cigarette in hand, his face pockmarked by the passions and boredom of Neapolitan youth, gazed with indifference or melancholy at the exaggerated depth of the sky. Listening carefully, one could hear snatches of song—*"cchiù bello 'e te"* or *"'o sole mio,"* "more beautiful than you," "my own sun"—but a silence persisted in the houses, as in the streets, that was not cheerful, as if the Christian celebration spreading temporarily over the anthill of streets were not so much a celebration as the flag of an unknown army raised at the center of a burned and devastated village. Dressed in his best, a boy of about thirteen, hands in his pockets, looked out from a balcony next to the Finizios' window, with the grave, yellowish face of the seriously ill, spitting while he daydreamed. From time to time, a dog passed by in a hurry.

"That life would have been a dream," Anastasia continued to think, trying to harden herself, to overcome that vague fear, that weakness and confusion of her thoughts, pierced by such an unusual and cruel light, "like a lane that seems to be trailing off out in a dirt field, and instead, unexpectedly, opens into a square full of people, with music playing. Suddenly, you see, I would go and live in a house of my own. I wouldn't go to the shop anymore. Yes, I never liked that life. I felt that someday it would have to end. Certainly I would get a satisfactory price for the shop. I can ask two million, even more, for that hole-in-the-wall in Chiaia. With two million, I could afford a place near here, so every day I'd come see Mamma. Three rooms and a terrace, with a view of San Martino." She saw herself busy in those rooms, on a summer morning, hanging out clothes, and singing. But although she remained glued to this image, she did not extract any joy from it. It was as if she were witnessing someone else's happiness. She thought also of summer evenings, when they would eat on the terrace, in the glow of an electric light hidden in the pergola; it would illuminate her hardened worker's hands on the table, and make Antonio's beautiful teeth sparkle in the darkness. And now thinking of those teeth, she saw, amazed, that all her intoxication originated there, in that mouth, younger than her own, indeed, young, with that health and youth that she had never possessed. And how had so many years passed—twenty, thirty—without her knowing this, without her wanting or even suspecting it? And why—now—did she desire it?

She calculated rapidly how old he was, thirty-two, and, comparing it to her own age, said aloud: "Impossible."

She was still looking down, but her face was different: her brow wrinkled in the effort to get control of herself, her pink eyelids lowering, with the mechanical movement of a doll, over eyes distressed by humiliation. In the face of that certainty, everything that was disagreeable about her came to the surface, like the foam on the sea. Impossible, impossible! And her lips tightened, her cheeks, of an orange-pink color, caved in, making her forehead appear larger and bleaker, and the arch of her eyebrows more pretentious. Terribly unhappy, the Finizios' older daughter had no expression, and her saddest moments were also the most perfectly banal. There was some obtuseness in her mind, that was all, a torpor, although sometimes she was aware of it, like the effect of an effort sustained over many centuries. She couldn't think, live. Something was alive in her, and yet she couldn't express it. This was her goodness, her strength, this incapacity to understand and want a life of her own. Only in remembering could she, from time to time, see, and then immediately that light, that landscape was extinguished. She remembered Antonio as if it were yesterday: not tall, but solid as a column, with brown hair and dark skin, and those sad eyes, of a man, and the mouth with the crowded teeth, white when he smiled; and the affectionate ways, as if marked by compassion, that he had with everyone, as if he were always returning from far away: "How are you, Anastasia?" "What do you want, life is the same … " "True, but it could be better." (And who knows what he was alluding to with that "better.") "Come and see us sometime, it would be a pleasure." That was all she knew to say to him, when they met, and with an idiotic, haughty expression. As if she were happy, as if her work were enough for her, and the satisfaction of supporting the whole family since her father died, and all those clothes that she made could console her. Instead, it wasn't true. Countless times she would willingly have thrown away all those satisfactions, and gone to be a servant in his house, and serve him, serve him forever, the way a true woman serves a man.

Bells tolled in two or three churches at once, and, at that terrible and familiar sound, which spoke of heaven and not of life, Anastasia roused herself. Her eyes filled with tears, and leaving the window she resumed walking up and down the room, her attention rapt, while she repeated mechanically: "The way a true woman serves a man ... Yes, nothing else."

"Anastasia! Anastasia!"

"Where is Anastasia?"

It was Anna and Petrillo. Her only sister, pale-faced at the age of eighteen, with the beauty of ordinary roses, her large, gentle, protruding eyes at that moment filled by a lively smile, and Petrillo, with his air of a studious cockroach, eyeglasses planted in the middle of his small green face, rushed into the room where Anastasia Finizio was pacing restlessly, absorbed in those new thoughts. In fact, the one who rushed in was Anna, in a white dress that spread around her narrow hips as she ran, one hand, almost out of habit, at her blond hair, tied by a blue ribbon. Petrillo, in a man's suit even though he was only sixteen, was a few steps behind, holding on to his eyeglasses, because one lens was broken and the least movement might cause it to fall out.

"Did you see who's arrived?"

"No," answered Anastasia, returning to the window and pretending to look out. She took off her gloves and put them back on, with her heart jumping out of her chest, and all of her aging blood rushing to her face, imagining she would hear, in a moment, that name. Never had she been so embarrassed. But she was wrong.

"Don Liberato, Donn'Amelia's brother, from Salerno. He sent someone to say that he's coming to see us after lunch."

"Yes?" said Anastasia, relieved to feel that her heart was beating more regularly, her head cooling. At the same time it was as if that shadow, that sadness which in all its extraordinary imaginings had continually emerged to obscure the colors, had solidified, and she sat down, like a beggar, on the chair in the corner of the room. Her agitation vanished suddenly, and she was able to look at her siblings.

"Why? Donn'Amelia isn't coming?" she asked calmly.

"She was sick all night," Anna answered, going to look at herself in the windowpane, with an indolence that was due not merely to southern frivolity but also to the languor of lifeless blood, "and the doctor came this morning, too. Didn't you hear?"

"Anastasia doesn't hear anything except money," said Petrillo maliciously, and he waited for an irritated response, but his sister said nothing.

"Mamma asks," Anna continued idly, "if you would take the green glasses with the gold trim out of the chest. Dora Stassano and Giovannino are coming for lunch."

This Giovannino was Anna's fiancé, a bookstore clerk, a short man with a red mustache, and although Anastasia didn't think much of him, her heart constricted as she thought how her sister, twenty years younger, could speak easily about things that instead caused her confusion and torment. Even the thought of having to bend over the chest in her mother's room, in her good clothes, to take out of its dusty interior the glasses so dear to Signora Finizio that she used them only on special occasions increased that inner chill. All Anna did was play the piano and take walks, for Anna duties … annoying things … didn't exist. A nice life, Anna's.

"Petrillo, go out a moment," she said in a flat voice.

"I've just done my nails," Anna said timidly. "I'm sorry."

Anastasia didn't respond this time, either. While the boy left, whistling, with the superior attitude he'd acquired some months earlier, ever since he'd started to exchange a few serious words with a girl, Anastasia took off her blue wool coat, which had seen all that great joy, and then those bewilderments, that suffering, and laid it on the bed. With the same care, she took the blue hat off her head, removing the pins first. She opened her purse, also blue, took out a very white, scented handkerchief, and held it for a moment under her nose. Finally she sat down on the bed and, without using her hands, took off her shoes, which she pushed aside. In doing all these things, she was wasting time; there was a kind of silence in her, and also an obscure apprehension. That moment of emotion minutes earlier had disappeared completely, vanished, and she felt her younger sister looking at her, in fact observing her, with the large, beautiful, slightly surprised eyes of youths destined to die prematurely (Anna had a weak lung), and she had a very faint sensation of shame, of guilt, as if she were already old, and all those fabrics, powders, and scents that she put on her person constituted a theft, a sin, something that was taken away from the natural need of her brothers, of Anna. A thousand years seemed to pass before her sister left the room, before she stopped looking at her.

"Mamma asks if you will also go to the kitchen for a moment and give them a hand. I have to look over the songs."

"Yes, I'm coming," Anastasia answered calmly. "I'm just going to rest a moment, then I'll come."

But her sister wasn't paying attention to her anymore. Near the open window, she was looking at her reflection in the glass, through which other balconies could be seen, and turning her pretty blond head slightly, she adjusted the blue ribbon and sang softly, *Tutto è passato!* It's all over! in her dull, gentle voice.

To get to the kitchen, Anastasia had to go out into a wide, bare hallway, onto which all four rooms of the house opened, and illuminated at the far end by a window looking onto a garden. Now that window was wide open, and the crudely whitewashed frame enclosed a dark blue sky so smooth and shining that it seemed fake. That morning an enormous beauty was in the air, and by comparison the houses and lives of men appeared strangely poor, shabby. And so Aunt Nana, who was hunched over, washing the floor, seemed to Anastasia's disturbed gaze a real monstrosity. This woman, her mother's older sister, after an idle youth, full of frivolous endeavors, and in continual expectation of a husband, had gradually had to resign herself, as happened among the women of the petty bourgeoisie, to a servile and silent life in the house of the married sister. Bring up this child, bring up this other one—there had no longer been time for personal occupations and thoughts. Over the years she had become almost completely deaf, so that she no longer grasped the scoldings or the laughter that from time to time came at her expense. Her obsession was newspapers, which she read avidly at night, lingering in particular on stories of passion, on the more prominent love stories: suicides and homicides for love, injuries, rapes, when there were not, as she preferred, notices of famous people's engagements, weddings of princes and rulers, and, in short, the luxury and beauty of the world, mixed in with the happiness of the flesh. Then everything in her puffy, false, putrid-yellow face lit up, making her terrible eyes even blacker and shinier: the eyes of a woman who hasn't been able to live, but still could, and there alone she could be heard chuckling: "Youth, ah, youth, what joy!" She had always been short in stature, but now she seemed more than short, shrunken and twisted, like ancient trees at the heart of some forest. She always wore black, and on Sundays and holidays she dabbed her cheeks with rouge. Seeing her, Anastasia felt that sadness, too confused to be defined, increase, that disgust and at the same time pity for herself and the life she lived, that mute longing for a sweeter day which had been whispering in her ear, and she said:

"Precisely this morning you have to be so dutiful, Aunt Nana? Don't you feel how cold it is?"

"Beautiful, beautiful," answered Nana, getting up humbly and all excited, her eyes on the window. She had understood "beautiful." "Very beautiful day," she said, "made just for the young." And again she lowered her gaze to the floor. Once, she would have envied Anastasia her height and her nice clothes, because as a young woman she had been peevish and mean. But life, confining her to the lowest positions, had triumphed over those flaws, and now there was no one humbler than Nana, and inclined to be satisfied by the happiness of others. For Anastasia, then, she felt true adoration. Ultimately, it was Anastasia, with her work, who maintained her, and who knows where she would have ended up, poor Nana, if God had not blessed Anastasia's work.

In his room, bleak and cold as his sister's, and, like it, cursorily furnished, Eduardo, the older brother, was shaving in front of a small mirror attached to the window. As tall as Anastasia, and terribly thin, he had a chest hollowed like the moon, resembling all those of his ilk. But now he was cured, although secretly he still coughed something up, and in fact he, too, was about to marry, not to mention that he had been promised a temporary position at City Hall. Having seen his sister passing in the mirror, he called out in a shrill, pleading voice:

"Anastasia, my shirts!"

"They're already ironed!" Anastasia answered. "Next to the socks."

And she was about to go on, when she noticed, as if seeing it for the first time, his long back, his flattened, feeble figure, and she thought of a half-desiccated spider that sometimes hung from a web and appeared to move in the wind, and then one realized it was only a shadow. Similarly, Eduardo lived the life of a man only in appearance. Here if you saw him shave and ask shrilly for his shirts, he was a man ... As her gaze fell on the two beds, Eduardo's and Petrillo's, she recalled that in two months they would be replaced by a single big bed. The expenses for the furniture were Dora Stassano's; she worked as a dressmaker and earned pretty well, but Anastasia, too, would contribute, and she and Dora Stassano would have to support the children who would come, with long backs and the faces of miniature old horses. Anna, on the other hand, was not making such a good marriage, because Giovannino Bocca, the clerk, would never earn much, but her mother, because of Anna's delicate health, and fearing that death would take her away before she could enjoy herself, was determined to make her happy: and Anastasia alone, with the help of that clerk, would have to support the little children, with faces white as a winter rose and slightly protruding, astonished eyes. But she didn't linger on that detail: as a workhorse has the sensation that his burden is increasing from minute to minute, and his legs are folding under him, but his gentle eyes can't look back, so she couldn't see from which direction this enormous and useless life flowed over her, and knew only that she had to bear it. She thought for a moment how different the rooms of the house would be in spring: here Eduardo with Dora; in the sisters' room Anna with her husband. She, Anastasia, would go and sleep with her mother, while Petrillo would be settled on a cot in the dining room. In the past, when her father was alive, no one would have foreseen these changes, no one would have thought that Eduardo and Anna, marrying, would stay in the house. She recalled suddenly how she liked her room, when she was younger, and the endless chatter with Anna, between the beds, on summer nights, with the moonlight on their feet, the low laughter when the name of this or that man was mentioned. Unnoticed, that whispering had ceased.

As she passed the black box of the intercom, it rang. "Hello," said Anastasia.

"Your brother's fiancée is here," the porter's voice informed her from below.

In that home (because they still didn't know what type Petrillo's girl was) the official fiancée was Dora Stassano. So Anastasia said right away:

"Dora Stassano, happy Christmas to you and all your family."

"Who is it? Doruccia? Tell her to come up," cried Eduardo with the shaving brush in hand, turning his feverish eyes toward her.

"Eduardo says come up if you want," Anastasia reported. And after a moment: "Yes, he's expecting you. We're all here. Anna and Petrillo, too." She hung up the intercom receiver. "She's coming," she said, turning toward Eduardo's room.

In the kitchen, all four burners of the stove had been lighted. There wasn't enough coal (the gas was used only for coffee), and Signora Finizio had needed to add some wood, which had filled the space with an acrid smoke. A ray of sun, entering through the open window, lightly rippled that massive gray veil upon which millions of colored spots sparkled. Her eyes red, half closed because they stung, Signora Finizio, a lively woman, all bone, with red hair and a shrewd, loving face, moved with incredible agility, given her fifty-eight years, from one burner to the next. Seeing Anastasia, she cried:

"Please, dear daughter, have a quick look at the broth, while I finish the kneading."

It seemed to Signora Finizio, sometimes, that Anastasia wasted time in futile things, but she didn't dare to protest openly, for it appeared to her that the sort of sleep in which her daughter was sunk, and which allowed them all to live and expand peacefully, might at any moment, for a trifle, break. She had no liking for Anastasia (her beloved was Anna), but she valued her energy and, with it, her docility, that practical spirit joined to such resigned coldness. She was always amazed that her daughter was so resigned, but of course it was part of God's plan.

Anastasia went to get an apron hanging behind a door, among the brooms, and she tied it in front. But instead of going to the stove she washed her hands at the sink, and said:

"You look at the broth, Mamma, I'll take care of the kneading."

"Thank you, dear daughter," the mother said, with a rapid smile; and for a moment stood looking at her, as her large hands plunged into the pond of water and flour, feeling that obscure sense of pity and celebration, of remorse and joy, that always gripped her upon observing Anastasia's perfect, unchangeable ugliness, her rigid, expressionless features, like those of a fork. She was silently comparing that ugliness with the memory she had of herself as a girl, with the image of Anna, so luminous in her weakness, and smiled without knowing it.

"Your sister doesn't want to do anything," she said aloud.

"Anna's young, Mamma," Anastasia answered without looking up, as if she felt that gaze. "And she's never been too healthy."

"That's also true," said Signora Finizio, full of emotion. And she added impulsively and with a tinge of melancholy, "So often I say to myself: What will become of that daughter of mine the day Anastasia wants to marry? Will the eyes of her husband be enough to protect her? Because, some time or other, that day may come."

"You're joking, Mamma," Anastasia said in a slightly altered voice. "I'm not pretty."

Signora Finizio smiled again, and as Anastasia, looking at her, had misinterpreted that smile, she didn't want to disappoint her, and changed the subject.

"Don Liberato sent the servant to tell me he is coming to see us after lunch. He's arrived from Salerno. Bless us, I think Donn'Amelia is very ill."

"May the Lord have mercy on her," Anastasia confined herself to saying.

Signora Finizio was never at rest. Like her arms, her thoughts were never still, and she needed to shift, always biting into this subject or that. So, after glancing at the broth, she turned and said:

"I also heard from the Lauranos that their son came back last night from Genoa. I didn't want to tell you because I thought you'd feel bad. It seems that he's also engaged."

And she quietly observed her daughter's long face, which had become horribly hard and unpleasant in her efforts to control herself. Signora Finizio's lips lengthened into a very thin smile. Her youth had quickly run its course, and she didn't easily forgive anyone who wished to avoid the law that she had been subjected to. She was constantly irritated by Anastasia's secret intentions, her lack of humility, by seeing her live so independently, almost a lady, while she herself led a servile life.

"It's better this way, don't you think?" she insisted.

Anastasia didn't answer; she went to the sideboard to get some flour, and for a few moments, although she wished to, Signora Finizio couldn't see her daughter's face. But she already knew she had hurt her enough.

"May I? Ooh, what smoke! Merry Christmas to all!"

Dora Stassano, in the kitchen doorway, showed her face, common, thin, and eager, the olive skin made greener by the red of her scarf. "Can I give you a hand?"

"Shoo … shoo …" Signora Finizio cried playfully. She somewhat regretted what she had said to Anastasia, but she remained cheerful. "Everybody out. When my daughter and I work we don't want anyone in the way."

Dora Stassano was a small woman in a bright-green coat trimmed with golden fur, wearing green gloves and shoes, and Anna's charming blond head, along with Eduardo's ugly smiling face, could just be glimpsed behind her.

"Mamma, will you let us see the dessert?" asked Eduardo.

"You, hurry up, if you don't want to miss the last Mass," his mother cried to him. "This family of mine is filling up with heretics," she said, turning to Dora. "Except Anastasia, who never fails in her Christian duties, and every morning peeks into church before she opens the shop. I want to know who honors God in this house. Look at him, at the age of thirty, he has to be led by the neck to the last Mass. And his siblings follow his example. At least you, Dora Stassano, have done your duty?"

"Last night we were all at Santa Maria degli Angeli, if that's what you mean," the girl answered.

"Good, good!" Like Nana, Signora Finizio was becoming a little deaf, and so she said even the most delicate things in a loud voice.

"The church was so crowded it was suffocating," Dora continued, in the contrite and mischievous tone of one who says things that, in essence, she doesn't care about but likes others to believe. "I didn't see you, Mamma, you must have been farther up front. But I saw the Torri sisters, then Donn'Amelia with her brother, and the servant behind, and when the Elevation came Donn'Amelia began weeping. More toward the front were the Lauranos, all of them, including the son."

There was a brief silence at that word "son."

The thought that Donn'Amelia, a good neighbor, was in her last days (she had a serious heart ailment) moved and at the same time cheered Signora Finizio, who in her meager existence drew obscure consolation from the misfortunes of others, and in fact was undecided for a moment whether to stay with that subject or the second. But the second was more important. She still didn't feel at ease concerning Anastasia's feelings.

"So, Antonio really is back?" she cried. "I'm pleased. And he's getting married?"

This question, who knows why, no one answered. The smoke in the kitchen, pierced by a thin ray of sun, glittered like gold. There was a sensation of happiness and of expectation in all of them, even, impossible as it might seem, in the unhappy Anastasia. And now advancing through that ray of sun, almost crawling on the floor, was the horrible body and the waxy smiling face of Nana. With comical gestures, leaning on her man's walking stick, she indicated that someone had come; like a dog, humble and content, she pulled on the motionless Anna's dress.

She finally understood.

"Oh, Giovannino!" she said, turning her head, suddenly animated and blissful. And she disappeared into the hall.

"They love each other, ah. They're in love. They're so in love. Fine thing, fine thing youth is," and, looking this way and that, Nana spoke by herself, as always, partly because no one paid attention to her, while Eduardo had sneaked away, in secret from his mother, to open the sideboard and see the dessert.

Taking advantage of that moment, Dora Stassano went up to Anastasia and, looking at her with eyes burning like black fire and encircled by just a thread of melancholy, said in an undertone:

"Greetings from Laurano."

Again the bells began to ring, but this time only in her mind. Anastasia cleaned her flour-covered hands on a rag and, head lowered, said coldly:

"Same to him."

"I know that you once entertained a thought," Dora said, staring at her.

"We were all young," Anastasia answered.

"He also told me that, one of these days, if he had time, he would stop by for a moment."

"He can come when he wants, it will always be a pleasure for us."

Signora Finizio, with her long pointed nose over the boiling pot, felt that around the table, in the smoke and cold of that holiday morning, there was a mood different from the normal one; she realized that Anastasia Finizio, even if her appearance was, as usual, indifferent and serious, was disturbed. With true anguish, she understood that the equilibrium, the peace of the family would be in danger if the pillar of that house softened. She would have liked to get rid of Dora Stassano, but she didn't want to fight with Eduardo, and then Dora was important. Nor was it good to annoy Anastasia. Humiliate her, she had to, that was all, humiliate her and, indirectly, delicately, recall her to her duties. In thinking this, she had to make an effort to repress a torrent of anger, and a hidden suffering (to this she was reduced, begging from her children), which suffocated her. Smiling, she turned to Dora:

"And Antonio, how was he? He's not coming to see us? At one time he did come."

"Yes, he told me that he'll come one day soon," Dora shouted in one ear.

"Ah, good, good!" said Signora Finizio, with an expression almost of lament. And, as she turned her gaze, seeing that Eduardo had taken the dessert down from the sideboard, and was furtively running a finger over it, then licking it, she shouted with savage irritation: "Get out, you shameless boy, get out!"

Eduardo obeyed, happy, partly because he knew that her shout wasn't directed at him, and he left the kitchen, pulling Dora Stassano along with him.

"I feel exasperated today, who knows why," Signora Finizio complained when she was left alone with Anastasia.

"You must be tired, Mamma."

"Maybe. These holidays are a terrible strain, only the young enjoy them. As for us, at our age, there's nothing that can bring us comfort. To serve, serve until death, that's what's left for us. Everything we do is for others."

In the dining room, the table was set with all the best silverware, plates, and glasses. There were eight places because Dora Stassano's only sister had also been invited, and with her Giovannino Bocca, Anna's fiancé. On the sideboard, among some bunches of pink flowers, the famous green glasses were lined up, twelve in all, and, farther back, the porcelain plate with the Sicilian cassata could be glimpsed. The fruit was arranged on a lower table.

But the most interesting thing was the crèche, an enormous construction of cardboard and cork. It was Eduardo's doing. Every year, with the eagerness of a child, he started work on it two months before the holiday, shrieking like a madman if someone disturbed him. This year, since things were going well for the family, it was bigger than ever before, taking up the whole corner between the balcony and the kitchen door, where usually there was a small console table with a scene of Venice above it. Because of this construction, the room seemed smaller and more cheerful. It really was a work carried out with painstaking and patient love, in which all a man's capacities and intelligence were on display. The background had been made from an immense sheet of royal-blue cardboard sprinkled with perhaps two hundred stars cut out of silver and gold paper, and attached with glue. The grotto, dug into the arc of an undulating, peaceful hill that somewhat resembled Naples, wasn't large, and you had to stoop down to make out the figures inside, which were barely thumb-size. St. Joseph and the Virgin, both molded with the rock they were sitting on, had bright pink faces and hands, and, bending over the manger, seemed to be grimacing horribly, like people who are dying. The child, much bigger than his parents (in part for symbolic reasons), was instead smooth and pale, and slept with one leg over the other, like a man. His face showed nothing, other than an apathetic smile, as if he were saying, "This is the world," or something like that. A tiny electric light illuminated the stable, where everything, from the child's flesh to the animals' noses, expressed passivity and a harsh languor.

Outside the grotto it was much more beautiful. The shepherds were a real army, motionlessly inundating that small mountain. They appeared to be going up and down the slopes, looking out of one of the white houses built into the rock (in the style of southern towns), or leaning over a well, or sitting at the table of a country inn; or, finally, to be sleeping, waking, walking, courting a girl, or selling (and you could see their mouths opened in a cry) a basket of fish, or resoling shoes (sitting at a cobbler's bench), or performing a tarantella, while another, crouching in a corner with a mischievous air, touched a guitar. Many, standing near a donkey or some sheep, had their arms raised to indicate a distant point in that blue paper, or shielded their eyes with one hand to protect them from the bright light of an angel, who had dropped from a tree, with a strip of paper on which was written "Hosanna!" or "Peace on earth to men of good will!" Finally, there were two elegant cafés, on the model of those in Piazza dei Martiri, with small nickel-plated tables on the sidewalk, and red-wheeled carriages that drove up and down, carrying ladies holding fans and white parasols.

Every so often someone stopped piously in front of that simulacrum of the Divinity, and observed this or that animal, or even picked one up—a sheep or a rooster—and examined it from all sides with curiosity.

The room was already full of family members, chatting as they waited for lunch, and the younger, like Petrillo and Anna, jokingly played some notes on the piano.

"Murolo is always Murolo," Eduardo was saying, while Anna, standing in front of the piano, played now this key, now that one, enunciating, with her mouth closed, the words of *Core 'ngrato*— Ungrateful Heart—the same that could be heard in the morning, rising here and there in the narrow streets from phonographs and radios:

Tutto è passato!

"That's enough, enough of these sad things," said Dora. "Today is supposed to be joyful. This is the year that everyone's getting married," she added, winking at Anastasia.

Anastasia, standing near the balcony, elegantly dressed, but with a long, melancholy expression, because she was still thinking of this life and of Antonio, gave her a glance full of gratitude and at the same time of anxiety, feeling herself revive yet again in those words. Therefore, she, too, was considered young; for her, too, there was hope! And that obstruction in her heart, that confused shame, that opposition to thinking things not suitable for her—maybe those were the mistake, and not the hope of living.

Aunt Nana's walking stick could be heard pounding everywhere. The poor woman, like a frog that happens into a circle of butterflies and no longer cares about the boredom of its existence, was eager to seize on some voice, a single note in that jumbled, gentle chatter, which would restore to her a connection with what she had long ago lost. Youth and love tormented her with curiosity, and she examined faces, unable to hear the voices, and muttered and laughed continuously, approving what she thought she grasped.

"Oh, oh, what joy, what beauty is youth!" On her yellow cheeks, in honor of youth, she had put a little rouge, and now her terrible eyes were burning. "Oh, oh, what joy!"

"As for me," Giovannino Bocca, a young man with a carrot-colored mustache and big red ears, was saying, "as for me, I think the Naples team is on its way to becoming good. But it needs money ... yeah ... a lot of money."

"Also, our stadium needs to be renovated ..." Eduardo observed, in a bored tone, and, approaching the piano, he moved some scores around on the music stand. "It seems that Casa Ricordi is having a revival. Have you heard what great songs they have this year?"

"Here's one that's pretty good for dancing," said Anna. "Listen ..."

"It really makes you want to dance," and Dora Stassano spun around vivaciously, while Petrillo observed her.

There was nothing extraordinary here. Anastasia knew and pitied the young, who were sickly and unemployed, with few ambitions, few dreams, a scant life; and yet, at that moment, they appeared to her beautiful, healthy, happy, rich in dreams and possibilities that would one day be fulfilled; and she shared in that joy, even though she knew that it didn't belong to her, that she was remote from it. Her brain knew this, but her blood no longer knew it. Now at any moment, the young man would arrive; the door would open and he would come right in, and, sitting at the table, without looking at her, would ask, a little self-conscious, a little emotional: "Well, how are we doing? And you, Anastasia, still at the shop? I heard you're getting married, too, is it true?" Oh, my God! Everything would change, after that conversation, the afternoon would be different from the usual, and the evening as well; maybe, talking to Anna in their room, late at night, she would tell her everything. And the next day would be another day, and the day after, too. The news would spread. "Anastasia's getting married ... It seems she's marrying the Lauranos' older son ... He's younger than she is, but men have these odd passions ... He'll never leave her ... He's jealous." No, jealous was too much, even if it warmed her heart. They would say, instead: "She's almost old, but he loves her just the same ... It was a feeling he'd had for years ... He admired her."

"To the table, to the table!" Signora Finizio cried just then, entering the room with a tray that held the steaming white porcelain soup tureen, full of the countless little yellow eyes of the broth.

With a great scraping of chairs, the table was soon occupied. Prayers were recited, good wishes repeated, and Anastasia felt a happiness so intoxicating and strange that, suddenly, without saying a word, she went around kissing everyone, mother, siblings, in-laws, and when she returned to her place, her eyes shining with tears, she couldn't breathe.

They had finished the appetizer, and were tasting the first tagliolini, with small sighs of satisfaction (only Anastasia, completely absorbed in her dream, had barely touched her spoon), when the contentedness and peace of that hour were pierced by an indescribable noise, a broad and secret wave of sounds, of sighs rising from the courtyard overlooked by the dining room balcony, and from the building's stairways and open loggia. Petrillo, who had jumped up to go and see, held his breath for a moment, then erupted in an excited "*Madonna!*" at which they all or almost all rose abruptly to go to the windows, while Nana, who, her mouth full, and intent on chewing, hadn't noticed anything, continued to repeat, "Oh, what joy, oh, what joy!"

In front of one of the two doors on the third floor, where Donn'Amelia lived, there was a small crowd from which rose weeping and laments. That weeping came from the servant and one or two neighbors, while the others confined themselves to remarking on the fate that had cut off the life of Donn'Amelia, still young.

In a rush, Eduardo opened the balcony door, and they all went out, despite the cold air, to see better. Indeed, all the tenants had done the same.

The balconies overlooking the courtyard were crowded with people who had interrupted Christmas lunch to observe with surprise and a certain disquiet how death had passed over that house, and on a holiday, too. Silence had fallen on the Finizio family, which was then broken by remarks such as:

"Who would have thought!"

"Poor Donn'Amelia!"

"Still, she was ill."

"Don Liberato was in time to see her."

From one person in the crowd came this message, directed toward a distant balcony: "She died with the blessing of the Holy Father!"

"Lucky her!" responded another voice. "Now her suffering is over."

"This life is a torment," another lamented.

"Punishment."

"Hear the bells!" (And in fact they were rumbling again, announcing the last Mass.) "They're ringing for her."

"She's no longer of this world."

"God rest her soul."

And the Finizio family, as if dazed, murmured:

"On this day!"

"Who would have expected it!"

"Now we must go and offer our condolences!"

"Certainly not," Signora Finizio burst out. "It wouldn't be polite. Close them! Close the windows! God rest her soul. Let's go back inside."

Turning, she bumped into Nana, who had come toward the balcony, and now, leaning on her stick, with her puffy face upturned, all confused, raised her big eyes questioningly.

"Who was it? Who was it?"

"Donn'Amelia is dead. God bless us!" her sister shouted in her ear.

"The bread? What does she want with the bread?" answered Nana, bewildered.

"Unstop your ears, aunt," Eduardo said harshly. "They haven't brought her any bread, in fact, she'll never eat any again. She died suddenly."

"Oh, oh, oh!" said the old woman, and her horrible, crimson-colored face darkened, her eyes lowered and filled with tears. That was life, one day or the next, when youth had gone: the poorhouse or a coffin.

Anastasia needed to go to her room to get a handkerchief. Her heart that day was as delicate as the strings of a violin, and vibrated if it were merely touched. She wept, not so much out of pity for the dead woman, whom she knew and respected, as out of tenderness for this life, which appeared so strange and profound, as she had never seen it, resonant with emotion. It was as if, for some hours, she had been drinking two or three glasses of wine all at once: everything was so new, so intense in its daily simplicity. Never, ever had she been so aware of the faces, the voices of her mother, her siblings, other people. That was why her eyes were full of tears: not because Donn'Amelia was lying on her deathbed, pale-faced and meek as she had always been, but because in this life there were so many things, there was life and death, the sighs of the flesh and despair, sumptuously laid tables and dirty work, the bells of Christmas and the tranquil hills of Poggioreale. Because, while downstairs they were lighting candles, a kilometer away was the port, where Antonio's ship was anchored, and Antonio himself, who had been so dear to her, at this hour was sitting at the table, with his relatives, thinking of who knows whom or what. And suddenly she realized that, amid so many emotions, her deepest thoughts had returned to being calm, cold, inert, as they had always been, and she no longer cared about Antonio or about life itself.

She didn't wonder why this was. She sat again on the bed, as she had that morning, and, looking calmly at the plainest and most familiar details of the room—the chairs, the old paintings, the dried olive branches against the white of the walls—she was thinking what her life would be like twenty years from now. She saw herself still in this house (she didn't see her own face), she heard the slightly irritated sound of her voice calling her nephews and nieces. Everything would be like today, on that Christmas in twenty years. Only the figures changed. But what would be different? They would still be called Anna, Eduardo, Petrillo, with the same cold faces, joyless, lifeless. They would be the same, even if in reality they had changed. Life, in their family, produced only this: a faint noise.

She was amazed, remembering the festive atmosphere of the morning, that budding of hopes, of voices. A dream, it had been: there was nothing left. Not for that reason could life be called worse. Life … it was a strange thing, life. Every so often she seemed to understand what it was, and then poof, she forgot, sleep returned.

The bell rang in the hallway, and right afterward steps could be heard, exclamations, animated voices, including Signora Finizio's, secretly victorious. "My dear lady, what a pity, have you heard?" It was the neighbor from next door, coming to borrow some coffee. On the street, which should have been deserted, two imbeciles were intently blowing into a bagpipe and because no other voice arose, no other sound, that sad and tender note spread everywhere, at times mingling with a light wind now meandering across the Neapolitan sky.

"Anastasia!" called Signora Finizio. Of course she needed something. "Anastasia!" she repeated after a moment.

Mechanically, in that torpor that had now taken over her brain and made her inert, Anastasia went to the closet, opened it, and, seeing the blue coat, which hung there like an abandoned person, delicately ran her fingers over it, feeling a compassion that wasn't, however, connected to anything, to any particular memory or suffering. Then, suddenly aware of her mother's call, she answered slowly, with no intonation:

"I'm coming."

1953

WHITE DOGS IN THE SNOW

Andrea De Carlo

We spent Christmas morning with my family and I had to tell them for the third time my stories about Rome and about the time I had spent with the author Marco Polidori. My sisters and my mother were curious, my father more skeptical in his indirect way. He was worried by the idea that I had left a secure position in an impulsive move to Rome; but I had never let him read any of my novel, and he had no idea of what possibilities might await me in that realm. It was Christmas, and in the end our thoughts tended to get lost in the exchange of gestures and gifts, in the various roles that we played, in the familial phrases we repeated over and over to the point of exasperation.

In all of this I was not able to stop thinking about Maria Blini: the fact that I was in a place I knew so well seemed to summon her up in my mind every few minutes, sending fresh and irregular currents through my heart. I knew almost nothing about her, nor did I have enough information on which to base any realistic expectations. It was exactly this that distracted me midconversation, filling me with a sudden anxiety and causing me to leap to my feet and head to the nearest window to look outside. My older sister remarked to my younger sister, "Isn't

Roberto acting strangely?" That she might have been able to intuit what was going through my mind was almost pleasing to me instead of disquieting.

Just before dinner I went down to the street with the excuse of making sure I hadn't left a present in the car. I ran like crazy to the nearest telephone booth but the phone was out of order; it spit my coins out as soon as I had thrust them in. I had to race back to the apartment as quickly as I could, dashing upstairs to my parents' place and arriving out of breath, to face Caterina's perplexed stare.

That evening I repeated the same scenario at her parents' house in the mountains after leaving a gift-wrapped book in the car on purpose as an excuse to leave. Once again I ran to the closest public telephone, the Swiss coins in my hand and my heart beating rapidly: this time the phone worked but at the other end of the line I heard only Maria's voice on the answering machine. I didn't leave any more messages for fear that she would listen to them all at once and think she was being stalked by a maniac; I didn't really have anything specific to say to her, nor could I leave her a number where she could call me back. I wondered what she was doing at that very moment, if she was in Rome or someplace else, if she was with her family or with Luciano Merzi with the slicked-back hair. I ran back across the icy snow, full of jealousy and impatience and desperation from the distance that separated us; I almost forgot the book, my alibi, that I'd left on the back seat of the car.

Caterina and I skied in the mornings, the ski runs full of people in the first snowy year after so long. In the afternoons and evenings we began our reading of Polidori's books; I had bought them all in Rome before leaving. It amazed me to think that he had read my one and only novel with the greatest of attention whereas I had only vague secondhand impressions of his works. I was suddenly taken by the desire to correct my embarrassing ignorance: I skied less and less and read more and more, from morning until late at night, almost one book each day, one after the other, in chronological order.

And in my ignorance I was surprised because Polidori's novels were much more vivid and interesting than I had ever imagined them to be. The first novels that he had written in his Argentinian period had a tautness that was almost experimental, the more recent works displayed a research of literary engineering that bordered on the overly aware, but the novels in between were full of color and enjoyment and passion. It seemed to me that this was the essence of his writing: the engagement, the well-developed characters and story lines, the feelings that took possession of the style and molded it to suit their inner breath. Page after page I was stupefied by the rich range of emotions and concrete situations which Polidori had depicted in his novels; I felt even more stupid and uncouth and uncultured for not having known this earlier, and for having brought him my attempt at an unfinished novel without any knowledge of his work.

I also tried to understand which of his stories were autobiographical or in some way based on real life; when it seemed to be the case I read with twice as much attention as before, drawn in by the complicated dance between men and women at the center of each story. My continual thoughts about Maria provoked in me a strange hypersensitivity as I attempted to decipher the fabric of attraction and innate impulses and rational thoughts and social mores to which Polidori returned time and again but always via a different angle of approach. From my protected vantage point of the chalet in Pontresina, the novels from his central period seemed to me to be infrared telescopes aimed squarely at life; I read them as if I could gain from them some essential information.

Caterina also read Polidori's books, and she also preferred the novels he had written in his thirties. She said to me, "One can feel that he wanted to write them. He had stories to tell, and it made him happy to tell them. After *The Mimetic Embrace* he became much colder and much more detached as an author." It was the only novel of his that I had read before meeting him and I assumed they were all very similar. She added, "It seems like he writes because he must, now, to maintain a certain standard and affirm his existence. He doesn't put his heart into it anymore."

She was right, even though Polidori's most recent novels were still full of precise and unconventional observations, and written in a language that was close to perfection. But they centered much more on the writing than on his usual vibrant contents, and they were constructed with a great deal of rational attention so that they seemed more like highly literary essays than actual novels. I wondered what had caused this change in him as an author and when it had taken place; if it was irreversible or just a phase he was going through. I wondered if it had been caused by disappointment, or because he had fallen out of love or if his energy had been diverted for external reasons.

In secret I tried again two or three times to call Maria Blini, then I stopped. I continued to think about her, but more often like some kind of exotic mirage. My relationship with Caterina was solid and had been for years: a lack of stimulation was mixed intimately with tenderness, boredom with reciprocal knowledge. We were not unhappy together in the cozy climate of Christmas and far away from everything else.

Then on the evening of January 3rd I was in my bedroom reading Polidori's *Breath of the Cicadas* with *Blonde on Blonde* by Dylan playing at low volume on the turntable, when Caterina's mother came to me to say excitedly, "Marco Polidori is on the phone!"

I got up to answer, almost bothered by the idea that two distinct areas of my life should come into contact in this way. But Polidori's voice was even warmer than the last time we had seen each other; the pleasure of talking to him again made thoughts and desires begin to flow in me once more.

He said, "Happy New Year, you old bastard." I answered, "Happy New Year to you, too, old bastard," In the living room Caterina's mother, father and brother all turned their heads, but I was pleased that they knew I was on such friendly terms with Marco Polidori.

He asked me if I had been working on my novel; I told him I hadn't. He said he hadn't been able to do anything he had wanted to either, he had been too busy with holidays and his children and a huge New Year's Eve party that Christine had insisted on throwing. It was strange to talk to him after having spent ten days reading his books; my mind was full of his settings, the rhythm of his sentences echoed in my ears; I felt as if I was seeing everything illuminated by his observations.

Polidori said, "Why don't you come down here, instead of staying in that Swiss old-age home? Bring your wife, it would be a pleasure for me to meet her. It will be another whole year before there are days like these."

There was an urgency in his voice, as if he knew that the circumstances he was referring to would never materialize again in the same way; deep down there was a hidden sense of delusion that I might not decide to take advantage of them while it was possible.

So I said to him, "All right, thanks," even though I thought that Caterina would want to spend the last two days in the mountains, and that her family would be offended to see us leave before our decided departure. But his tone was infectious, and I was agitated at the thought of having to stay where I was.

Polidori replied, "Great, Roberto," and he seemed very happy; he explained to me how to arrive at his house in the country.

It took us nearly seven hours to make our way from Pontresina to Florence in our beat-up old Volkswagen, and another hour from Florence to the tiny village in the hills that Polidori directed us to. When we arrived it was dark; we went into a bar to call him, exhausted by the difficult drive of hundreds of miles, our heads and bodies throbbing from mechanical vibrations.

Christine Polidori answered the phone with her usual courteous tone; she gave me her husband right away. Polidori said, "We were about to send out a search party, we thought you'd lost your way." He told us to stay close to the bar, he would come and get us right away. He said, "I'm really glad that you're here, Roberto."

We waited in the bar for about ten minutes, then we went outside to wait for him in the *piazzetta* where we had left our car, just outside the walls of the city It was a small medieval town with its stone buildings perfectly preserved; it seemed very beautiful under the nighttime lights, but we didn't attempt to visit it for fear of missing Polidori. Caterina stamped her feet in the cold, looked around, and said, "When is he coming?" I explained to her that he was never very punctual; "I can see that," she replied. But she was curious to meet him; she had left her parents' house in the mountains without any qualms.

I was very glad she was with me, as she had been for almost all of the travels of my adult life, and at the same time I felt less liberated than I would have wished to. With her next to me it seemed more difficult to be different from the me she knew so well: I felt as if I had a witness and guarantor by my side for a version of me that I would have liked to change, and this thought unnerved me. But I loved her, and bringing her with me compensated in some small way for my feelings of guilt regarding Maria Blini, and for all of the territory that Maria Blini had taken over inside of me: for the diversity of occasions and desires and possibilities that Marco Polidori had opened up in front of me and that I wished to explore on my own. We walked back and forth across the piazzetta, our eyes following the infrequent headlights that appeared along the road without communicating our thoughts to each other.

I was also wondering if Polidori's lack of punctuality stemmed from his artistic nature or if there were other reasons for it: if he used it to create a slight feeling of insecurity in those who had to wait for him, discouraging any requests of him that might seem too direct. I wondered if by chance we had ended up in the wrong town or at the wrong bar, or if I would have to call him back.

But in the end he appeared and as soon as I saw him I assumed a perfectly casual air, as if I could have waited another hour for him without being upset by it at all. It wasn't something I did knowingly; it was an instinctive reaction to what I thought he might have expected of me.

He pulled up in an old Land Rover covered in mud instead of the usual unbranded green automobile he drove when he was in Rome. He was wearing a lined, waxed field jacket and farmer's boots. They made him look quite different than he normally did, but he did not look like he was wearing a country costume; he maintained his usual slight distraction about material goods.

This time he apologized for being late: he said, "Sorry, but I got a call just as I was heading out the door. This bombastic imbecile of a mayor insists on giving me an honorary citizenship of the city of Bordeaux. Who knows why, what on earth do I have to do with Bordeaux?"

He took Caterina's hand in the gallant way that I had already observed when we were at a party in Rome; he said to her, "You are even more beautiful and more Milanese than Roberto describes you to be in his book."

"That's not her in the book," I insisted, much too weakly.

Polidori replied, "Very well, but she is very beautiful and very Milanese all the same." He continued to look at her in the same way one would admire a work of art; as if his admiration was as noble as the object he admired, without being at all insistent or intrusive.

Caterina said to him, "Now you are embarrassing me," but she smiled in a way that showed she was pleased by his compliments, and the tone of her voice was more tender and frivolous than that of the young woman doctor she normally used in public.

Polidori greeted me as well, saying, "You old bastard, it's good that you came." We gripped each other energetically in that man-to-man hug we had codified when we first met, the time he came to pick me up at my residence in the hills outside of Rome.

Then he said, "All right, I'll lead the way." He looked at Caterina again, and asked her, "Would you like to ride with me, and Roberto can follow?" He said to me, "Do you mind, Roberto?"

I replied, "No, no," and at any rate Caterina was already heading toward the Land Rover, turning back only for a second to look at me.

We drove away from the town and followed a small country road for a few miles that curved and rose and fell according to the undulations of the land. I kept the red rear lights of the Land Rover in sight, and I wondered what Caterina and Polidori were talking about. There was snow on the hillsides, and lights here and there from small villages and isolated homes, but it was too dark to see anything else.

After about seven miles or so Polidori left the paved road and turned on to a hard dirt road that rose between a line of cypress trees on either side. I had trouble following him up the steep hill, the old Volkswagen slipping and sliding in the mud laced with wet snow. At a certain point the car stopped altogether; I slammed on the horn like mad, afraid that Polidori and Caterina would drive away and leave me where I was. Polidori drove back and pulled out a steel cable and hooked it to my car. He did it quickly, with a manual dexterity I did not expect; he said, "It happens all the time, don't worry." Caterina peered at me through the back window with a level of curiosity she might have had for a stranger; even if I had almost never been jealous of her in seven years, I felt a flash of anger that she chose to go with Polidori instead of with me. Polidori slid back behind the wheel of his Land Rover and pulled me to the crest of the hill like a load of scrap metal.

We stopped at the top, but could not see anything of the house except for the external lights on a wall of lightly-colored stone. We got out of our cars and immediately two enormous, white dogs arrived to greet Polidori and to growl deeply at me and Caterina. Polidori said to them, "They're friends. Friends!" and he touched my arm and Caterina's arm to demonstrate. He pressed their large muzzles against our legs. The two dogs sniffed us and Polidori said, "Don't worry, they only maul enemies," and he opened the front door.

Once inside the outer walls we realized that it was not simply a house but an ancient monastery that had been remodeled, with a loggia, a garden and elegantly arched windows that looked out over the greenery. After such a long trip on the highway and the last miles in the dark and muddy cold, it was a kind of vision: a dream with harmonious and proportionate lines, illuminated by warm light. Caterina and I stood in the entryway with the same stunned expression on our faces; neither of us could find the right words to express our thoughts in that moment.

Polidori realized this and he played it down; he said, "When I bought it twelve years ago I thought I had made an incredibly idiotic choice."

"Because it was so run-down?" I asked him, trying to regain my confidence.

"Pretty much," he replied. "It was dead, really. It's a place that needs to have a lot of life in it in order to be happy. It must be full of light and sounds and human and animal warmth, and then it's all right."

It was not a large monastery, anyway: there must not have been very many monks or nuns originally, and this rendered the space even more cozy. Polidori had restored it without letting himself be constrained by rules: there were colorful rugs on the floors and large modern paintings on the walls, and an efficient heating system. He led us down a corridor, toward a room from which came voices and music. Every few steps, Caterina would comment, "*Incredibile.*" Polidori asked, "Do you really like it?" as if he was not already sure about it himself.

His family was in a large living room, full of light and of sounds and human and animal warmth, exactly as he had said. His three children were running around the room and playing with an electric train set, Maggie, the nanny, and his wife, Christine, were sitting near a large fireplace; a boy with dark, shaggy hair was reading on a couch, there were three more dogs of various sizes in addition to the two large, white ones that had followed us in; and music was emanating from a magnificent stereo.

Christine Polidori got up to greet us; Polidori introduced her to Caterina, and he introduced the other people in the room. The boy with dark hair was his son from his first marriage, and his name was Roberto, too. He was very different from the three new children who were blond and almost Nordic, but his eyes and the shape of his nose were those of Polidori; it was shocking to see them standing next to one another. Polidori noticed the expression on my face when I realized that the boy had the same name as I did, and he smiled. The boy looked at me without pretending to be cordial; he did not shake my hand. He was maybe seventeen or eighteen years old; he had a wild and diffident air about him and was dressed in old jeans and beat-up tennis shoes, almost contrasting on purpose with the evident respectability of his three younger siblings.

Caterina and I exchanged some semiformal conversation with Christine, then Polidori took us to our room. Along the corridor he said, "It's such a relief you're here. We had some unbearable guests until yesterday morning; I felt like running away and leaving them on their own."

Before taking us upstairs he gave us a brief tour of the monastery-house: he showed us the kitchen, a music room, a gym, and a small covered swimming pool; there was also a room with fragments of a fifteenth-century fresco on the ceiling. He opened the doors as if he did not wish to brag about these spaces that filled us with so much admiration. At a certain point he said, "I don't know if you can tell, but twelve years ago I really believed in it, when I was just beginning to fix it up. I was trying to put together a kind of ideal house, I think. Now it's Christine who takes care of it, and she does a very good job, it has become hers."

But it was easy to see that he was not at all indifferent to the house, as he would have liked us to believe: all we had to do was look at him while he showed us a secret passageway or an interesting window, or the small hothouse where the aromatic herbs were grown.

Caterina was completely taken with him, and there was no longer any trace of the bias she demonstrated in Milan when I told her about the first time I met him. She smiled when he spoke; she asked to know more about the architecture of the ex-monastery; she listened to him with an attentiveness that she had hardly ever shown toward me. Polidori, on his part, spoke more to her than he did to me, and found infinite fascinating details to describe to her; he would place his hand lightly on her arm to show her something. As we entered the library he said to me, "Do you know, Roberto, that you have a very charming wife, you undeserving old bastard?"

I answered, "I know," although just a second before I was thinking how much I would have wanted to be there with Maria Blini instead, combining the unlimited fascination I felt for her as a person yet to be discovered with that of the place. I was pleased that Polidori was so enthusiastic about Caterina, and it made me nervous, too: I was tense and tired from the trip, and confused by my conflicting emotions.

In the library the shelves were filled with every kind of technical book: dictionaries and encyclopedias and historical and geographical atlases, instruction books for automobiles and cameras and pistols, manuals on how to raise rabbits and how to cultivate freshwater pearls, writings on pediatrics and horticulture and beekeeping, volumes about magnetic waves and iridology, about the history of the crusades and the Tartars and the area of Tuscany that we were in. Polidori saw that I was looking at some telephone books from foreign cities, and he said to me, "I use them for names, every once in a while." There weren't very many novels, and almost all of them were old; very few were published after the 1950s.

Our room was beautiful, with two arched windows looking out over the loggia where the Italian garden opened onto a vegetable garden that led to a field that ran all the way to a dark forest. Polidori showed us everything we might need and then left us alone, telling us to come downstairs whenever we were ready. As soon as the door closed Caterina looked at me with shining eyes and said, "Marvelous."

"Polidori?" I asked.

She replied, "The place, you boob. But Polidori, too, yes. He's much better than I thought he would be."

"Why? How did you think he would be?" I asked her, as I looked at the antique wooden bed and I imagined being able to sleep there with Maria Blini.

Caterina replied, "I don't know, more the important author, full of himself. And also more obsessive: the great seducer. Maybe because I had *The Mimetic Embrace* in my mind and I thought the main character was a kind of self-portrait."

While my feelings were conflicted I was proud that she knew I was his friend and that he respected me as an author, and that I had access to his private life including invitations to his house in the country.

Dinner was very good, almost all of the dishes were made from food grown on the grounds, with everything being prepared by a Tuscan woman. There was no trace of the punitive rigor present when I ate at their house in Rome, still the atmosphere was not relaxed. There was a web of tension between Polidori and his wife and the English nanny and the children and young Roberto: glances loaded with resentment, sentences full of thinly veiled anger. The children played with their food, the nanny scolded them in her coarse Cockney accent; young Roberto ate with his head down like a stranger who had been taken in off the street; Polidori's wife complained of the Italians' inability to produce a legible train schedule; her husband looked at her with hatred. Caterina seemed oblivious; she tried to make conversation in her polite way, even when no one was listening to her. This made me so nervous that I kept interrupting her, furious at her lack of perception and at the intertwined tensions of the others; I cut her words off midway.

Polidori attempted every once in a while to make us feel at ease; he would make an observation or a joke or find a story to tell, but perhaps this was the only audience in all of Italy that was insensitive to his talents as a raconteur. His son Roberto seemed particularly hostile to him. He leaned on his elbow in a way that horrified Christine, and when Polidori spoke to him he did not reply. Caterina asked him which school he went to, making me nervous with her renewed efforts to be polite. Roberto Polidori answered in a half-whisper "high school" without meeting her eyes.

Polidori said, "Ever since he was six I've been telling him that high school is useless, it would be a thousand times better for him to follow a specific course of study." Christine said, "Specific in what way, when he is still so young?" The nanny squeaked at the children, "Don't leave the table until you have permission!" Caterina commented, "What a beautiful piece of furniture you have against the far wall."

When dinner was over Polidori asked me if I wanted to get some air; we went out under the loggia without putting our coats on, walking on the snow to the far end of the garden. The two giant, white dogs came with us, running back and forth as we walked.

Polidori said to me, "Another terrible dinner, Roberto. I'm sorry."

"It was delicious," I said, trying not to make anything of it.

"I didn't mean the food," he said dryly. He was examining the overcast sky; he said, "We put together this perfect scene like it's from a postcard, with everything exactly in place, and underneath there is so much exasperation that we're no longer able to talk to each other."

I said to him, "It happens to every family, especially around the holidays. You should have seen my parents' house on Christmas Day."

He didn't answer me; he said, "My older son hates me, each time we see each other it gets worse. He has never forgiven me for leaving his mother, he thinks I'm some kind of assassin."

I asked him, "When did you separate from your first wife?" We were headed toward the darkness of the forest, and because he brought the topic up I didn't have any qualms about being direct.

He said, "I left when Roberto was five years old. Twelve years ago, now." He pulled a stick out of the snow and threw it for the dogs to chase, but the dogs weren't able to find it and they came back, looking at us expectantly. He continued, "It must not have been easy growing up with a ghost for a father: he calls every night but only shows up every two or three months, and you see him on television and in the newspapers but he's never there when you need him."

The big, white dogs continued to run around, their paws crunching on the frozen snow. I imagined Polidori's past life in many different ways, scattered and transformed by the stories from his novels that I had read recently.

Polidori said, "And before I left it was probably worse, because I spent my time fighting fiercely with his mother. I don't think he has great memories of that." He laughed in the darkness, walking with long strides. He said, "Good God, the compressed anger there was between us. I remember one time when we fought in a hotel in Paris: at a certain point I grabbed her by the neck and wanted to strangle her for how inflexible her reasoning seemed to be. I could have done it. I realized in that moment exactly how it can happen, how one does not have to be a criminal. And Roberto was there in the room with us; he was crying like crazy."

"Do you think he remembers?" I asked him, trying to imagine him in such a violent situation.

Polidori replied, "Maybe he doesn't remember that particular time, but all of the episodes together influenced his behavior toward me. Every time he looks at me it seems he wants to blame me for something, even if he never talks about anything specific. He has this way of acting, as if he considers me directly responsible for everything that he doesn't like about himself, his life and the world."

"But it's always that way, isn't it?" I said to him. "I mean, at his age."

"Maybe," replied Polidori. "But it doesn't make me feel any less guilty. I know for certain that he would probably find something to hold against me even if I had remained in the family home, as a model husband and father. But then all I need to do is see him again, and I am reminded of everything I made the three of us go through. The evasions and lies and the multi-layered thoughts that tormented me every minute of every day when I was with them. The time I stole from him to give to other people, people I don't even remember anymore."

I said to him, "Still there are many ways not to be present. For example my father never left home but he had no idea how to communicate with me, or he never really tried. If I think about it, I realize that we never talked about anything important, even though he was always there, I saw him every day."

"I know, I know," replied Polidori. "And your father would probably have a lot of things to blame his father for, seeing that it's his fault if your father was never able to talk to you. It's an infinite chain of unresolved affections and wrong circumstances and impossibility to communicate, but it doesn't make you feel any less remorse about it all."

"I can imagine," I said to him, and I wondered which of his novels told the story of a childhood that corresponded to his actual childhood.

Polidori said, "Children don't grow up in a linear fashion. They move ahead in fits, in ways you can't predict. You go away for a month or two and when you return they're different people, with capabilities and attitudes completely different from those you knew. All of a sudden you have no idea how to approach them. They see things they had no interest in before, and they've lost interest in what used to excite them. With Roberto I missed everything, and I realized it the entire time. I tried to concentrate into two days what I hadn't done in months, but I knew it was useless. And still I couldn't do anything about it; I needed to be out and about, and to be free."

"On the other hand, you're close to your younger children," I added. I was cold without my coat; I was wondering how much farther he would want to walk.

"No," said Polidori. "Maybe it's the resentment that my oldest son feels for them that latches on to me like a virus, but sometimes I feel as if I don't love them at all. It makes me angry that they take everything for granted; having a family, an organized home, constant attention and objects and toys and presents and clothes and food and everything they need and don't need. Sometimes I look at them, and they are so disgustingly spoiled. I feel like grabbing everything from their hands and kicking them out in the cold for a little while. They seem to have slow reflexes, lulled by the ease of their lives. Every so often I imagine them grown up, three more stupid children of a famous parent."

I said to him, "Doesn't it seem a little early to say that, poor things?" But it was true that there was something irritating in the way they seemed to have stepped out of an ad for biscotti and milk.

"It's not early," said Polidori. "If you had seen Roberto at their age, he was another species altogether. Even if now he won't talk unless you twist his arm, you should see his drawings. Hardship is what develops intelligence, and ease produces only a lack of motivation and slow reflexes. The children belong to Christine much more than they do to me, in any case. I am just their financial sponsor and the engine behind it all, for the most part they get along fine without me. There is a kind of unwritten contract between us, an agreement about a certain level of performance with respect to the rest of the world, and roles to fulfill."

By now I could not understand how much he might be exaggerating, or how much he might be influenced by the darkness and the cold all around us.

He was quiet for a moment, then he stopped and said to me in a different tone, "Poor Roberto, not only was it a terrible dinner, but then I drive you crazy with my conversation."

I said to Polidori, "It's not true, this is interesting to me." A slight breeze was picking up, my food was becoming frozen in my stomach.

Polidori replied, "You're polite, but as a writer you should never be. A writer should never put up with any kind of boredom. He should shout, 'Enough!' as soon as he feels harassed and tell everybody to go to hell."

I laughed, my arms wrapped tightly around my chest as I looked at the monastery-house illuminated in the dark night.

"Race you?" Polidori said, and we took off running, back toward the light and the warmth and the tensions of his family, with the great, white dogs galloping beside us.

1991

THE GOLDEN CROSS

Grazia Deledda

It was nearly Christmas Eve, I was supposed to write a story for a foreign newspaper for the occasion, and I still hadn't found my subject.

Then it occurred to me to go gathering folktales (I still lived in Sardinia at the time).

I knew an old man who had a good store of them: he was a sharecropper on one of our parcels in the valley. In summer and in fall he would walk uphill, bent over his cane, a saddlebag filled to bursting and slung over his back, his beard tucked into the saddlebag's pocket. He almost always came late in the afternoon, as the stars smiled down on us children from the lilac sky at twilight. The old man seemed to us like one of the Magi who had lost his way and strayed from his companions. The saddlebag was filled with things more precious to us than gold and myrrh: fruits and children's stories.

But in winter he didn't come, or came only rarely, and these visits didn't interest us, because he brought olives, and olives are bitter.

And I went down to find him: in the winter, the valley is pleasant, sheltered as it is. The clouds stretch out over it like a veil over a crib, the water recedes, and the cliffsides are dry. If the weather is fine, it feels like spring, and the almond trees blossom, in thrall like dreamers to the warmth, and the olives gleam amid the grasses like purple pearls.

The old man lived in a quaint hut built against an embankment, looking down on the olive grove, sheltered by brush and rock. He also had a primitive beehive, and the wild cats used to mount its hollow cork trunks, beautiful as miniature tigers.

There we were: the sun scorching the grounds, the olives silver, and the afternoon so luminous you could see rivulets glimmer on the mountainside and women picking up acorns in the grass.

The old man had laid out the olives to dry in the yard and was throwing out those that looked off. He didn't feel like talking; solitude and silence had rusted his tongue.

But the servant had brought a good medicine to loosen the knotted words, and the old man took a drink and started to complain.

"What stories do you want me to tell you? I'm old, and nowadays should only talk with the earth, which is already calling me. If you want stories, best to look for them in books, you know how to read."

"Drink a little more," the servant said, bending over, like him, to sort through the olives, "and then tell us about the time you were supposed to get married!"

"That's a true story, not some tall tale; yeah, I'll tell you that one, because it was right around now, at Christmastime, when it happened.

"I was twenty at the time, I was engaged. I was a bit young to be taking a wife, but things were bad, I had lost my father, and my mother was always ill; she was heartsick, but she was tranquil and God-fearing and used to tell me: 'Get married, so when I die, you won't have to bear life's cross all on your own, and you won't fall into the hands of the first girl who comes along.' We wondered: Who should I choose? I wasn't rich, and didn't have a mind to be so; it was enough for me if the woman was honest and God-fearing, too. And I thought and thought: Who will it be?

"There was a very respectable family, a father, a mother, seven hardworking children who all went to Mass and confession as God commands. Three of the seven were girls, beautiful, tall, slender, with thin waists, and they walked with lowered eyes, corsets laced up, hands tucked under their aprons, not like you all, the girls of today, who seem to eat everyone up with your stares. My mother asked for the youngest one for me, the offer was well taken, and at Christmas I was to give her a present. According to custom, that meant I was marrying her, and that she had agreed to marry me. And we thought and thought, my mother and I, about what this present should be: seated face-to-face in front of the fire, we argued long and hard: Should it be a gold coin, an embroidered scarf, or a ring?

"Finally, my mother said: 'Listen, boy, my days are numbered, and each step I take pulls me further from the things of this earth. Take my golden cross and give it to her.' And she gave it to me, with the nacre rosary it hung from. But when she did, her eyes welled with tears and her mouth fell open from heartache; I pitied her, and made to give it back, but she reached out to push back my hand, unable to say a word.

"I wrapped the cross and the rosary in a kerchief, then in a second kerchief, and kept it in my pocket for three days, like a relic. Now and then I would touch it, afraid to lose it, and I don't know why, I felt my heart swell with love, but also with a mysterious foreboding.

"On Christmas Eve, I went to the home of my bride to be. The other two daughters' suitors were there, and with all those people, the kitchen felt like a fairground. But everyone was serious, because the mother and father, with their serene but imposing faces, demanded respect, like saints on an altar; and the girls came and went, with lowered eyes, serving wine and sweets to their suitors and responding plainly, without smiling, to their compliments.

"I felt at ease, because I was a serious boy, an orphan, and took a stern view of life; all I needed was to look up now and again at my wife-to-be, and if, turning her back to her father and mother, she gave me a quick glance, for me it was as if heaven had opened up, and the kitchen with her parents, the suitors, the brides, and the brothers carving the lambs for dinner were like the celestial court with God, the saints, and the angels. How happy I was that evening! Never in my life have I been so happy. I was anxious for Mass to be over, so I could give my gift to my bride, and in that way bind myself to her. Then someone outside knocked at the door to the courtyard. One of the brothers went to open, and returned with a tall man in tow: a stranger with a small satchel slung around his neck and a goad in his hand that he used for a cane.

"I took a good look at him as he walked forward slowly, in light, flat shoes like they wear in Oliena. At first he struck me as ancient, with his short, white beard and his pale eyes; but then I saw he was young and blond, and weary, as if he'd come from far away.

"None of us knew him, and even the girls observed him with curiosity; but everyone figured he was a friend of the father, who greeted him warmly, though without much emotion. 'Have a seat,' he said, 'where are you coming from?'

"The unknown man joined us, not removing his bag, laying the goad across his knees and stretching his feet out toward the fire: he looked at each of us vaguely and smiled, as if we were old acquaintances. 'I've come from afar; I'm just passing through,' he said, his voice calmer than the father's had been. 'Since you're celebrating, I thought I'd stop in.' 'Yes, we're celebrating, as you can see: the girls are engaged, and look at their men here, strong and handsome as lions. You couldn't ask for more,' the father said. 'Not a thing more,' the boys shouted, nudging one another with their elbows, and then they all laughed.

"The girls, too, after all that seriousness, seemed overcome by a fulsome sense of joy; they laughed and laughed, and I laughed, too, and their mother and father laughed along with us: it was like a sickness passed from one to the others. Only the stranger stayed calm, looking at me like a child, unsurprised and unbothered.

"Finally, when everyone was serious again, he said, turning to the women: 'Many years ago, I passed through this country, and I entered a house with a couple engaged, just as I am doing now. The people were just as happy; but the bride-to-be gazed at me, and when I was leaving she followed me to the door, and said: You are my true bridegroom, I was waiting for you, stay and give me your gift. I did, and though I left and she married the other, I was forever her true husband, and her son will give to you young brides the gift I gave to her, and you will give it to your sons, and they in turn will give it to their brides.' We looked at one another, neither smiling nor laughing: the man struck us as strange, almost mad, and after our revelry, inspired suspicion, almost fear.

"My mother-in-law asked him: 'Do tell then, what was your gift?' 'A cross of gold.' Then I felt a shiver up my spine. The son of the stranger's lover could only be me. For I alone had brought my bride-to-be a golden cross, the one that belonged to my mother. I didn't say a word, but from then on, a thick veil seemed to be covering my head: I could see, but confusedly, and my ears were ringing, and I no longer understood the words the stranger, the mother, and the boys exchanged.

"I felt a deep pain, a heavy weight, a weight that crushed my kidneys, as though the golden cross in my pocket had suddenly grown massive and was bearing down on my back.

"Then the stranger, having warmed his feet, departed, tall and silent, with his pack around his neck and the goad in hand. 'Who was that?' the mother asked. 'Who knows?' the father replied. 'I've never met him, but he looks familiar. I must have seen him, years back, perhaps when he came in secret to visit his beloved.' I said nothing.

"Again, everyone was composed, serious, grave: the girls came and went, serving the dinner, but my bride, now pale, kept her eyes lowered, and would no longer look at me. My heart pounded, and through the veil I spoke of that enveloped my head, I seemed to see the eyes of young and old turn toward me with misgivings.

"And so it was, till the time for Mass came. We stood, but I felt worse, buckled beneath my weight, and staggered forward like a drunk. We walked in a line, the women in front, the men behind. Once in the church, we mingled with the crowd, and slowly, I pulled away, withdrawing to the stoup, then to the door, and finally outside … and there, I turned my back to the house of God and fled as though chased by demons.

"I walked like a madman, turning this way and that, until dawn; at dawn, I returned home. My mother was already awake. She was lighting the fire and looked tranquil but pale, as if she hadn't slept all night. Seeing me distraught, she assumed I was drunk, and laid out the straw mat to put me to bed. All she said was: 'Some impression you made, my poor boy!'

"I lay down, gnawed the straw mat; then I got on my knees, took out the golden cross, twisted it, and the beads bounced on the floor and rolled away: they seemed to be afraid of me. My mother, too, began to gasp.

"I took pity on her, and told her everything. 'What could I have done?' I shouted. 'The visitor's lover, the stranger's lover, was you—and I was supposed to give that cross to my bride? They all looked at me, they had guessed it: I ran away in shame.

"My mother was calm; she gathered the beads in her apron and began to thread them once more. She left me to fall silent; then she said: 'And why couldn't the other two have been the sons of the stranger's lover?' 'Because they had gold coins to give their brides, not crosses ...' 'The coins have crosses on them, too,' she said, 'Listen. The stranger passes through the home of all the brides-to-be and leaves a cross with every one of them. Do you think the three girls didn't go after him last night? Of course they did, and they got their cross, and their sons will be his sons, too. How simple you are!' she said, seeing my perplexity. 'Do you not believe in God? Yes, you believe in God and Christ, and you know that Christ isn't dead. He lives forever, and in the world, with us, and wanders without end, and he goes into the homes and blesses those who have given him alms, multiplying their loaves of bread; he blesses those who are good of heart, and turns their water into wine; and to every wife he gives a cross: of gold, but still, a cross! It was him, and you're a simpleton, and you didn't recognize him!'

"And so the cross," the old man finished, "remained with me."

1913

BLACK BREAD

Giovanni Verga

Neighbor Nanni had hardly taken his last breath, and the priest in his stole was still there, when the quarrel broke out among the children as to who should pay the costs of the burial, and they went at it till the priest with the aspersorium under his arm was driven away.

For Neighbor Nanni's illness had been a long one, the sort that eats away the flesh off your bones and the things out of your house. Every time the doctor spread his piece of paper on his knee to write out the prescription, Neighbor Nanni watched his hands with beseeching eyes, and mumbled, "Write it short, your honor; anyhow write it short, for mercy's sake."

The doctor carried out his own job. Everybody in the world carries out his own job. In carrying out his, Farmer Nanni had caught that fever down there at Lamia, land blessed by God, producing corn as high as a man. In vain the neighbors said to him, "Neighbor Nanni, you'll leave your bones on that half-profits farm!"

"As if I was a baron," he replied, "to do what I like and choose!"

The brothers, who were like the fingers on the same hand as long as their father lived, had now each one to think for himself. Santo had a wife and children on his back; Lucia was left without any dowry, as good as turned on the street; and Carmenio, if he wanted to have bread to eat, would have to go away from home and find himself a master. Then the mother, who was old and ailing, didn't know whose business it was to keep her, for none of the three children had anything at all.

The oxen, the sheep, the store in the granary had all gone with their owner. There remained the dark house, with the empty bed, and the equally dark faces of the orphans. Santo carried his things across, with Redhead, his wife, and said he'd take his mamma to live with him. "Then he won't have to pay rent," said the others. Carmenio made up his own bundle and went as shepherd to Herdsman Vito, who had a piece of grazing land at Camemi; and Lucia threatened to go into service rather than live with her sister-in-law.

"No!" said Santo. "It shan't be said that my sister has to be servant to other folks."

"He wants me to be servant to Redhead," grumbled Lucia.

The great question was this sister-in-law who had driven herself into the family like a nail. "What is there to be done, now I've got her?" sighed Santo shrugging his shoulders. "I should have listened in time to that good soul, my father."

That good soul had preached to him: "Leave that Nena alone, for she's got no dowry, nor house, nor land."

But Nena was always at his side, at the Castelluccio farm; whether he was hoeing or mowing, she was there gathering the corn into sheaves, or removing the stones from under his feet with her hands; and when they rested, at the door of the great farm-place, they sat together with their backs to the wall, at the hour when the sun was dying over the fields, and everything was going still.

"Neighbor Santo, if God is good you won't have lost your labors this year."

"Neighbor Santo, if the harvest turns out well, you ought to take the big field, down on the plain; because the sheep have been on it, and it's rested for two years."

"Neighbor Santo, this winter, if I've time, I want to make you a pair of thick leggings to keep you warm."

It was while he was working at Castelluccio that Santo had gotten to know Nena, a girl with red hair, daughter of the keeper, whom nobody wanted. So for that reason, poor thing, she made a fuss of every dog that passed, and she denied herself the bread from her mouth in order to make neighbor Santo a present of a black silk stocking cap, every year at Saint Agrippina's Day, and to have a flask of wine for him, or a piece of cheese, when he arrived at Castelluccio. "Take this, for my sake, Neighbor Santo. It's the same as the master drinks." Or else: "I've been thinking, you never had a bit of something to eat with your bread—not all last week."

He didn't say no, but took everything. The most he ever did was to say out of politeness: "This won't do, Neighbor Nena, you deny your own self to give to me."

"I like it better for you to have it."

And then, every Saturday night when Santo went home, that dear departed soul used to tell him again: Leave that Nena alone, for she hasn't got this; leave that Nena alone, for she hasn't got the other.

"I know I've got nothing," said Nena as she sat on the low wall facing the setting sun. "I've neither land nor houses; and to get together that bit of linen I've had to go without bread to eat. My father is a poor keeper, who lives at his master's charge, and nobody wants to saddle himself with a wife without a dowry."

Nevertheless the nape of her neck was fair, as it usually is with red-haired people; and as she sat with her head bowed, all those thoughts heavy inside it, the sun glowed among the golden-colored hairs behind her ears, and lit on her cheeks that had a fine down like a peach; and Santo looked at her flax-blue eyes, and at her breast which filled her stays and swayed like the cornfield.

"Don't you worry, Neighbor Nena," he said. "You won't go short of husbands."

She shook her head, saying no; and her red earrings that were almost like coral caressed her cheeks. "No, no, Neighbor Santo. I know I'm not beautiful, and nobody wants me."

"Look though!" said he all at once, as the idea came to him. "Look how opinions vary! They say red hair is ugly, and yet on you now it doesn't strike me as bad."

The good departed soul, his father, when he saw that Santo was altogether smitten with Nena and wanted to marry her, had said to him one Sunday: "You want her whether or not, that redhead? Say the truth, you want her whether or not?"

Santo, with his back to the wall and his hands behind him, didn't dare to raise his head; but he nodded yes, yes, that he didn't know what to do with himself without the redhead, and it was the will of God it should be so.

"And have you given it a thought as to how you're going to keep a wife? You know I can give you nothing. But I've one thing to tell you, and your mother here will say the same: Think it over before you go and get married, for bread is scarce, and children come quick."

His mother, crouching on the stool, pulled him by the jacket and said to him, sotto voce, with a long face: "Try and fall in love with the widow of Farmer Mariano, she's rich, and she won't ask a great deal of you, being part paralyzed."

"Oh yes!" grumbled Santo, "You may bet Farmer Mariano's widow would take up with a beggar like me!"

Neighbor Nanni also agreed that Farmer Mariano's widow was looking for a husband as rich as herself, lame though she was. And then there'd have been that other misery to look forward to, seeing your grandchildren born lame as well.

"Well, it's for you to think about it," he repeated to his son. "Remember that bread is scarce, and children come quick."

Then toward evening on St. Bridget's Day, Santo had met the redhead by chance, as she was gathering wild asparagus beside the path, and she blushed at seeing him as if she didn't know quite well that he had to pass that way going back to the village, and she dropped down the hem of her skirt that she had turned up around her waist for going on all fours among the cactus plants. The young man looked at her, also went red in the face, and could say nothing. At last he began to stammer that the week was over and he was going home. "You've no messages to send to the village, Neighbor Nena? Tell me if I can do anything."

"If I'm going to sell the asparagus, I'll come along with you, and we'll go the same way," said Redhead. And he, as if stupefied, nodded yes, yes; she added, with her chin on her heaving bosom: "But you don't want me, women are a nuisance to you."

"I'd like to carry you in my arms, Neighbor Nena, carry you in my arms."

Then Neighbor Nena began to chew the corner of the red handkerchief she wore around her head. And Neighbor Santo again had nothing to say; but he looked at her, and looked at her, and changed his saddlebag from one shoulder to the other, as if he couldn't find words to begin. The mint and the marjoram were making the air merry, and the side of the mountain, above the cacti, was all red with sunset. "You go now," Nena said to him. "You go now, it's late." Then she stood listening to the crickets rattling away. But Santo didn't move. "You go now, somebody might see us here by ourselves."

Neighbor Santo, who was really going at last, came out again with his old assertion, and another shake of the shoulder to settle his double sack, that he'd have carried her in his arms, he would, he'd have carried her if they'd been going the same road. And he looked Neighbor Nena in the eyes, and she avoided his looks and kept on seeking for the wild asparagus among the stones, and he watched her face that was as red as if the sunset were beating upon it.

"No, Neighbor Santo, you go on by yourself, you know I'm a poor girl with no dowry."

"Let us do as Providence wishes, let us—"

She kept on saying no, that she was not for him, and now her face was dark and frowning. Then Neighbor Santo, downcast, settled his bag on his shoulder and moved away, with bent head. But Redhead wanted at least to give him the asparagus that she had gathered for him. They'd make a nice little dish for him, if he would eat them for her sake. And she held out to him the two corners of the full apron. Santo put his arm around her waist and kissed her on the cheek, his heart melting inside him.

At that moment her father appeared, and the girl ran away in a fright. The keeper had his gun on his arm, and didn't see at all what should prevent him from laying Neighbor Santo out for practicing this treachery on him.

"No! I'm not like that!" replied Santo with his hands crossed on his breast. "I want to marry your daughter, I do. Not for fear of the gun; but I'm the son of a good man, and Providence will help us because we do no wrong."

So the wedding took place on a Sunday, with the bride in her holiday dress, and her father the keeper in new boots in which he waddled like a tame duck. Wine and baked beans made even Neighbor Nanni merry, though his case of malaria was strong; and the mother took out of the chest a pound or two of worsted yarn which she had put aside toward a dowry for Lucia, who was already eighteen, and who combed and arranged her hair for half an hour every Sunday morning before going to Mass, looking at herself in the water of the washbowl, for a mirror.

Santo, with the tips of his ten fingers stuck in the pockets of his coat, exulted as he looked at the red hair of his bride, at the yarn, and at all the celebration that there was for him that Sunday. The keeper, with a red nose, hobbled inside his shoes and wanted to kiss them all around, one after the other.

"Not me!" said Lucia, sulky because of the yarn they were taking from her. "This isn't water for my mouth."

She stayed in a corner pulling a sulky face, as if she already knew what her lot would be the moment her parents were gone.

And now sure enough she had to cook the bread and sweep the house for her sister-in-law, who as soon as God sent daylight set off for the field with her husband, although she was again with child, she being worse than a cat for filling the house with little ones. There was more needed now than presents at Christmas and at St. Agrippina's Day, or than the pretty talk she used to have with Neighbor Santo at Casteluccio. That swindler of a keeper had done well for himself marrying off his daughter without a dowry, and now Neighbor Santo had to see about maintaining her. Since he'd gotten Nena he saw that there wasn't bread enough for the two of them, and that they'd got to wring it out of the earth at Licciardo, by the sweat of their brow.

As they went to Licciardo with the double bag over their shoulder, wiping the sweat from their foreheads on their shirtsleeves, they had the young corn always in their mind and in front of their eyes; they saw nothing else but that between the stones of the path. It was to them like the thought of one who is sick and whom you have always heavy on your heart, that corn; first yellow, swamped in mud with all the rain; and then, when it did begin to get a bit of a hold, came the weeds, so that Nena had made pitiful work of both her hands, pulling them out one by one, bending down over all that load of her belly, drawing her skirt above her knees so as not to hurt the corn. And she didn't feel the weight of her child, or the pains of her back, as if every green blade that she freed from the weeds was a child she had borne. And when at last she squatted on the little bank, panting, pushing her hair behind her ears with both her hands, she seemed to see before her the tall ears of June, bending over one above the other as the breeze touched them; and they would count up, she and her husband, as he was untying his soaking gaiters, and cleaning his hoe on the grass of the bank: So much seed they had taken, and therefore they'd have so much corn if the ear came to twelvefold or to tenfold or even to sevenfold; the stalk wasn't very stout but the growth was thick. If only March was not too dry, and if only it didn't rain except when rain was needed! Blessed Saint Agrippina must remember them! The sky was clear and the sun lingered in gold on the green meadows, from the fiery west, whence the larks fell singing on to the clods, like black dots. Spring was really beginning everywhere, in the cactus hedges, in the bushes of the little road, between the stones, on the roofs of the hamlets green with hope; and Santo, walking heavily behind his companion, who was bent beneath the sack of straw for the animals, with all that belly on her, felt his heart swell with tenderness for the poor thing, and went along talking to her, his voice broken by the steep climbs, about what he'd do if the Lord blessed the corn up to the last. Now they didn't have to talk anymore about red hair, whether it was beautiful or ugly, or any such nonsense. And when treacherous May came with its mists to rob them of all their labors and their hopes of harvest, the husband and wife, seated once more on the bank watching the field going yellow under their eyes, like a sick man departing to the other world, said not a word, their elbows on their knees and their eyes stony in their pale faces.

"This is God's punishment!" muttered Santo. "That sainted soul my father told me how it would be."

And into the hovel of the poor penetrated the ill-humor of the black, muddy little road outside. Husband and wife turned their backs on each other, stupefied, and they quarreled every time Redhead asked for money to buy necessities, or whenever the husband came home late, or when there wasn't enough wood for the winter, or when the wife became slow and idle with her childbearing; long faces, ugly words, and even blows. Santo seized Nena by her red hair, and she set her nails in his face; the neighbors came running up, and Redhead squealed that that villain wanted to make her have a miscarriage, and that he didn't care if he sent a soul to hell. Then, when Nena had her baby, they made peace again, and Neighbor Santo went carrying the infant girl in his arms, as if he had fathered a princess, and ran to show her to his relations and his friends, he was so pleased. And for his wife, as long as she was in bed he made her broth, he swept the house, he cleaned the rice, he stood there in front of her to see that she wanted for nothing. Then he went to the door with the baby at his shoulder, like a wet nurse; and to anybody who asked him, as they were passing, he replied: "It's a girl, neighbor! Bad luck follows me even here, and I've got a girl born to me. My wife couldn't do any better than that."

And when Redhead got knocks from her husband, she turned around on her sister-in-law, who never did a hand's turn to help in the house, and Lucia flew back at her saying that without having any husband of her own she'd got all the burden of other folk's children foisted on her. The mother-in-law, poor thing, tried to make peace in these quarrels, repeating: "It's my fault, I'm no good for anything now. I eat idle bread, I do."

She was no good for anything but to hear all those miseries, and to brood over them inside herself; Santo's difficulties, his wife's crying, the thought of her other son far away, a thought that stuck in her heart like a nail; Lucia's bad temper, because she hadn't got a rag of a Sunday frock and never saw so much as a dog pass under her window. On Sundays, if they called her to join the group of gossips who were chattering in the shadow, she replied with a shrug of the shoulders: "What do you want me to come for? To show you the silk frock I haven't got?"

Sometimes however Pino the Tome, him of the frogs, would join the group of neighbor women, though he never opened his mouth, but stood with his back to the wall and his hands in his pockets, listening, and spitting all over the place. Nobody knew what he came for; but when Neighbor Lucia appeared in the doorway, Pino looked at her from under his eyes, pretending to be turning to spit. And at evening, when all the street-doors were shut, he went so far as to sing her little songs outside the door, making his own bass for himself—hmmm! hmmm! hmmm! Sometimes the young fellows of the village going home late, recognizing his voice, would strike up the frog tune, to mock him.

Meanwhile Lucia pretended to be busying herself about the house, as far as possible from the light, her head sunk, so that they shouldn't see her face. But if her sister-in-law grumbled, "There goes the music!" she turned around like a viper to retort: "Even the music is a trouble to you, is it? In this galley-hole there mustn't be anything for eyes to see nor ears to hear, my word!"

The mother who noticed everything, and who was also listening, watching her daughter, said that as far as she was concerned that music made her feel happy inside herself. Lucia pretended not to understand anything. Yet every day, at the time when the frog fellow was due to be passing, she did not fail to be standing in the doorway with her distaff in her hand. The Tome, as soon as he got back from the river, went around and around the village, always returning to that particular quarter, with the remains of his frogs in his hand, crying, "Song fish! Song fish!" As if the poor folks of those mean streets could afford to buy song fish!

"But they must be good for sick people!" said Lucia, who was dying to get a start bargaining with the Tome. But the mother wouldn't let them spend money on her.

The Tome, seeing Lucia watching him from under her eyes, her chin on her breast, slackened his pace before the door, and on Sunday he summoned enough courage to draw a little nearer, till he came so far as to sit on the steps of the next terrace, with his hands hanging between his thighs; and he told all the women in the group about how you caught frogs, how it needed the devil's own cunning. He was more cunning than a red-haired ass, was Pino the Tome, and he waited till the goodwives had gone away to say to Neighbor Lucia, "We want rain badly for the corn, don't we!" Or else, "Olives will be scarce this year!"

"What does that matter to you? You live by your frogs," Lucia said to him.

"You listen here, my dear friend; we are all like the fingers on one hand; or like the tiles on the roof of the house, one sending water to the other. If there's no crop of corn or of olives, there'll be no money coming into the village, and nobody will buy my frogs. You follow what I mean?"

That "my dear friend" went sweet as honey to the heart of the girl, and she thought about it all evening long as she was spinning silently beside the lamp; and she turned it around and around in her mind, like her spool that spun from her fingers.

The mother seemed as if she read into the secrets of the distaff, and when for a few weeks no more songs had been heard in the evening, and the frog seller had not been seen going past, she said to her daughter-in-law: "How miserable the winter is! We don't hear a living soul in the neighborhood."

Now they had to keep the door shut, for the cold, and through the little opening they never saw a thing except the window of the house across the road, black with rain, or some neighbor going home in his soaking wet cloak. But Pino the Tome never showed his face, so that if a poor sick person wanted a drop of frog broth, said Lucia, there was no telling how you were going to get it to her.

"He'll have gone to earn his bread some other road," said the sister-in-law. "It's a poor trade, that is, and nobody would follow it who could do anything else."

Santo, who had heard the chatter on Saturday evening, made his sister the following speech, out of love for her: "I don't like this talk about the Tome. He'd be a fancy match for my sister! A man who lives on frog catching, and stands with his legs in the wet all day long! You ought to get a man who works on the land, so that even if he owned nothing, at least he'd be drawn from the same class as yourself."

Lucia was silent, her head lowered and her brows knit, biting her lips from time to time so as not to blurt out: "And where am I going to find a man who works on the land?" How indeed was she to find him, all by herself? The only one she had managed to find now never showed his face anymore, probably because Redhead had played on her some nasty trick, envious, tattling creature that she was. There was Santo who never said anything but what his wife said, and she, the Redhead, had gone around repeating that the frog man was a good-for-nothing, which bit of news of course had come to the ears of Neighbor Pino.

Therefore squabbles broke out every moment between the two sisters-in-law.

"The mistress here isn't me, that it isn't," grumbled Lucia. "The mistress in this house is the one who was clever enough to wheedle around my brother and snap him up for a husband."

"If I'd only known what was coming I'd never have wheedled around him, I wouldn't, brother or no brother; because if I needed one loaf of bread before, now I need five."

"What does it matter to you whether the frog catcher has got a proper trade or not? If he was my husband, it would be his business to look after keeping me."

The mother, poor thing, came between them to soothe them down; but she was a woman of few words, and she didn't know what to do but run from one to the other, clutching her hair with her hands, stammering:

"For mercy's sake! For mercy's sake!"

But the women took not the slightest notice of her, setting their nails in each other's faces after Redhead had called Lucia that bad word, "Nasty-cat!"

"Nasty-cat yourself! You stole my brother from me!"

Then arrived Santo, and gave both of them knocks to quiet them, so that Redhead, weeping, grumbled: "I say it for her own good! Because if a woman marries a man who's got nothing, troubles come fast enough."

And to his sister, who was screaming and tearing her hair, Santo said, to quiet her: "Well what do you expect, now that she is my wife? But I'm fond of you and I speak for your own sake. You see what a lot of good we've done ourselves by getting married, us two!"

Lucia lamented to her mother: "I want to do as much good for myself as they've done for themselves! I'd rather go out to service! If a mortal man does show his face around here, they drive him away." And she thought about the frog catcher of whom there was never a sign nowadays.

Afterward they got to know that he had gone to live with the widow of Farmer Mariano; even that he was thinking of getting married to her; because though it was true he hadn't got a proper trade, he was none the less a fine piece of a young fellow, built without any sparing of material, and as handsome as San Vito in flesh and blood, that he was; and the lame woman had property enough to be able to take what husband she liked and chose.

"Look at this, Neighbor Pino," she said. "This is all white things, linen and everything; these are all gold earrings and necklaces; in this jar there are twelve gallons of oil; and that section is full of beans. If you like you can live with your hands in your pockets, and you needn't stand up to your knees in the marsh catching frogs."

"I should like it all right," said the Tome. But he thought of Lucia's black eyes looking for him under the cotton panes of the window, and then of the hips of the lame woman, which wobbled like a frog's as she went about the house showing him all her stuff. However, one day when he hadn't been able to get a scrap of anything for three days and had had to stay in the widow's house, eating and drinking and watching the rain fall outside the door, he persuaded himself to say yes, out of love for daily bread.

"It was for the sake of my daily bread, I swear to you," he said with his hands crossed on his breast, when he came back to look for Neighbor Lucia outside her door. "If it hadn't been for the hard times, I wouldn't have married the lame woman, I wouldn't, Neighbor Lucia!"

"Go and tell that to the lame woman herself," replied the girl, green with bile. "I've only got this to say to you; you don't set foot here anymore."

And the lame woman also told him that he wasn't to set foot there anymore, for if he did she'd turn him out of her house, naked and hungry as when she had taken him in. "Don't you know that, even more than to God, you're obliged to me for the bread you eat?"

But as her husband he went short of nothing: well clad, well fed, with shoes on his feet and nothing else to do but lounge in the marketplace all day, at the greengrocer's, at the butcher's, at the fishmonger's, with his hands behind his back and his belly full, watching them buy and sell.

"That's his real trade, being a vagabond!" said Redhead. And Lucia gave it to her back again, saying that if he did nothing it was because he'd got a rich wife who kept him. "If he'd married me he'd have worked to keep his wife." Santo, with his head in his hands, was thinking how his mother had told him to take the lame woman himself, and how it was his own fault if he'd let the bread slip from his mouth.

"When we're young," he preached to his sister, "we have these notions in our heads, like you have now, and we only think of pleasing ourselves, without counting what comes after. Ask Redhead now if she thinks folks ought to do as we have done."

Redhead, squatting on the threshold, shook her head in agreement with him, while her brats squealed around her, pulling her by the dress and the hair.

"At least the Lord God shouldn't send the plague of children," she said fretfully.

As many children as she could she took with her to the field, every morning, like a mare with her foals; the least one inside the bag over her shoulder, and the one a bit bigger she led by the hand. But she was forced to leave the other three at home, to drive her sister-in-law crazy. The one in the sack and the one that trotted limping behind her screamed in concert the length of the rough road, in the cold of the white dawn, and the mother had to pause from time to time, scratching her head and sighing: "Oh, my Lord!" And she breathed on the tiny blue hands of the little girl, to warm them, or she took the baby out of the sack to put it to her breast as she walked. Her husband went in front, bent under his load, and if he turned half around, waiting to give her time to overtake him, all out of breath as she was, dragging the little girl by the hand, and with her breast bare, it wasn't to look at the hair of Redhead, or at her breast which heaved inside her stays, like at Castelluccio. Now Redhead tipped out her breast in sun and frost, as if it served for nothing more except to give out milk, exactly like a mare. A real beast of burden, though as far as that went her husband could not complain of her: hoeing, mowing, sowing, better than a man, when she pulled up her skirts, and was black half-way up her legs, on the corn-land. She was twenty-seven years old now, with something else to do besides think of thin shoes and blue stockings. "We are old," said her husband, "and we've got the children to think of." But anyhow they helped each other like two oxen yoked to the same plough, which was what their marriage amounted to now.

"I know only too well," grumbled Lucia, "that I've got all the trouble of children, without ever having a husband. When that poor old woman shuts her eyes at last, if they want to give me my bit of bread they'll give it, and if they don't they'll turn me out onto the street."

The mother, poor thing, didn't know what to answer, and sat there listening to her, seated beside the bed with the kerchief around her head and her face yellow with illness. During the day she sat in the doorway, in the sun, keeping still and quiet till the sunset paled upon the blackish roofs opposite, and the goodwives called the fowls to roost.

Only, when the doctor came to see her, and her daughter put the candle near her face, she asked him, with a timid smile:

"For mercy's sake, your honor, is it a long job?"

Santo, who had a heart of gold, replied: "I don't mind spending money on medicine, so long as we can keep the poor old mother here with us, and I can know I shall find her in her corner when I come home. Then she's worked her share, in her own day, and when we are old our children will do as much for us."

And then it happened that Carmenio had caught the fever at Camemi. If the master had been rich he'd have bought him medicine; but Herdsman Vito was a poor devil who lived on that bit of a flock, and he kept the boy really out of charity, for he could have looked after that handful of sheep himself, if it hadn't been for fear of the malaria. But then he wanted to do the good work of giving bread to Neighbor Nanni's orphan, hoping by that means to win over Providence to his help, as it ought to help him, if there was justice in heaven. How was it his fault if he owned nothing but that bit of grazing land at Camemi, where the malaria curdled like snow, and Carmenio had caught the ague? One day when the boy felt his bones broken by the fever, he let himself sink asleep behind a rock which printed a black shadow on the dusty little road, while heavy flies were buzzing in the sultry air of May, and in a minute the sheep broke into the neighbor's corn, a poor little field as big as a pocket handkerchief, already half eaten up by the hot drought. Nevertheless Uncle Cheli, who was curled up under a little roof of boughs, cherished it like the apple of his eye, that corn-patch that had cost him so much sweat and was the hope of the year for him. Seeing the sheep devouring it, he cried: "Ah! You Christians don't eat bread, do you?"

And Carmenio woke up under the blows and kicks of Uncle Cheli, and began to run like a madman after the scattered sheep, weeping and yelling. Carmenio, who had his bones already broken by the ague, stood badly in need of that cudgeling! But he thought, did he, that he could pay in squeals and laments for the damage done to his neighbor?

"A year's work lost, and my children without bread this winter! Look at the damage you've done, you assassin! If I skin you alive it won't be as much as you deserve."

Uncle Cheli went round getting witnesses to go to the law with the sheep of Herdsman Vito. The latter, when he was served with the summons, felt as if he was struck with paralysis, and his wife as well. "Ah, that villain of a Carmenio has ruined us all! You do somebody a good turn, and this is how they pay you back! Did he expect me to stop there in all the malaria and watch the sheep? Now Uncle Cheli will finish us off into poverty, making us pay the costs." The poor devil ran to Camemi at midday, blinded by despair, because of all the misfortunes which were raining down on him, and with every kick and every punch on the jaw he fetched Carmenio he stammered, panting: "You've brought us down to nothing! You've landed us in ruin, you brigand!"

"Don't you see how sick I am?" Carmenio tried to answer, parrying the blows. "How is it my fault, if I couldn't stand on my feet with fever? It got me unawares, there, under the rock."

Nonetheless, he had to make up his bundle there and then, and say good-bye to the five dollar-pieces which were due to him from Herdsman Vito, and leave the flock. And Herdsman Vito was downright glad to catch the fever again, he was so overwhelmed by his troubles.

Carmenio said nothing at home, when he came back empty-handed and empty-bellied, with his bundle on a stick over his shoulder. Only his mother grieved at seeing him so pale and wasted, and didn't know what to think. She learned everything later from Don Venerando, who lived just near and also had land at Camemi, next to the field of Uncle Cheli.

"Don't you tell anybody why Uncle Vito sent you away," said the mother to her boy. "If you do, nobody will take you on as a hired lad." And Santo added as well: "Don't say anything about having Tertian fever, because if you do nobody will want you, knowing you're ill."

However, Don Venerando took him for his flock at Santa Margherita, where the shepherd was robbing him right and left, and doing him more hurt even than the sheep in the corn. "I'll give you medicine myself, and so you'll have no excuse for going to sleep, and letting the sheep rove where they like."

Don Venerando had developed a kindly feeling toward all the family, out of love for Lucia, whom he used to see from his little terrace when he was taking the air after dinner. "If you'd like to give the girl as well I'll give her half a dollar a month." And he said moreover that Carmenio could go to Santa

Margherita with his mother, because the old woman was losing ground from day to day, and with the flock she would at any rate not lack for eggs, and milk, and a bit of mutton broth, when a sheep died. Redhead stripped herself of the best of anything she had worth taking, to get together a little bundle of white washing for the old woman. It was now sowing time, and they couldn't come and go every day from Licciardo, and winter, the season of scarcity of everything, would be on them again. So now Lucia said she absolutely would go as servant in the house of Don Venerando.

They put the old woman on the ass, Santo on one side and Carmenio on the other, and the bundle behind; and the mother, while she let them have their way with her, said to her daughter, looking at her with heavy eyes from her blanched face: "Who knows if we shall ever see one another again? They say I shall come back in April. You live in the fear of the Lord, in your master's house. Anyhow you'll want for nothing there." Lucia sobbed in her apron, and Redhead did the same, poor thing. At that moment they had made peace, and held their arms around each other, weeping together.

"Redhead has got a good heart," said her husband. "The trouble is we aren't rich enough to be always fond of one another. When hens have got nothing else to peck at in the fowl house, they peck at one another."

Lucia was now well settled in Don Venerando's house, and she said she never wanted to leave it till she died, as folks always say, to show their gratitude to the master. She had as much bread and soup as she wanted, a glass of wine every day, and her own plate of meat on Sundays and holidays. So that her month's wages lay in her pocket untouched, and at evening she had also time to spin herself linen for her dowry on her own account. She had already got the man ready to hand, there in the selfsame house: Brasi the kitchen man who did the cooking and also helped in the fields when necessary. The master had got rich in the same way, in service at the baron's, and now he was a Don, and had farmland and cattle in abundance. Because Lucia came from a respectable family that had fallen on evil days, and they knew she was honest, they had given her the lighter jobs to do, to wash the dishes, and go down into the cellar, and look after the fowls; with a cupboard under the stairs to sleep in, quite like a little bedroom, with a bed and a chest of drawers and everything; so that Lucia never wanted to leave till she died. Meanwhile she turned her eyes on Brasi, and confided to him that in two or three years she'd have a bit of savings of her own and would be able to "go out into the world," if the Lord called her.

Brasi was deaf in that ear. But Lucia pleased him, with her eyes as black as coals, and the good flesh she had on her bones, and for her part she liked Brasi, too; a little, curly-headed fellow with the delicate cunning face of a little fox-dog. While they were washing dishes or putting wood under the boiler he invented every kind of roguery to make her laugh, as if he was trying to rouse her up. He squirted water on the back of her neck, and stuck endive leaves in her hair. Lucia squealed, in a subdued manner, so that the masters shouldn't hear; she took refuge in the corner by the oven, her face as red as fire, and she threw dishrags and twigs in his face, while the water trickled down her back like a thrill.

"With meat you make rissoles—I've made mine, you make yours."

"I won't," replied Lucia. "I don't like these jokes."

Brasi pretended to be mortified. He picked up the leaf of endive, which she had thrown at him, and stuck it in his bosom, inside his shirt, grumbling: "This belongs to me. I don't touch you. It belongs to me and is going to stop here. Don't you want something from me, to put in the same place, you?" And he pretended to pull out a handful of his hair to offer her, sticking out the length of his tongue as he did so.

She punched him with the solid punches of a peasant woman, which made him hunch up his back, and gave him bad dreams at night, he said. She seized him like a little dog by the hair, and found a certain pleasure in thrusting her fingers in that soft, curly wool.

"Keep it up! Keep it up! I'm not touchy like you, and I'd let myself be pounded to sausage meat by your hands."

One day Don Venerando caught him at these games, and made the devil of a row. He wasn't going to have carryings-on in his house; he'd kick them both out if there was any more of it. And yet when he found the girl alone in the kitchen he took her by the chin and wanted to caress her with two fingers.

"No! No!" replied Lucia, "I don't like those sort of carryings-on. If you don't leave me alone I'll get my things and go."

"You like them from him all right, you like them from him. And yet not from me who are your master? What do you mean by it? Don't you know I can give you gold rings and gold earrings with pendants, and make you up your dowry if I like."

Certainly he could, Brasi assured her, for the master had any amount of money, and his wife wore a silk mantle like a lady, now that she was old and thin as a mummy, for which reason her husband came down to the kitchen to have his little joke with the maids. And he came as well to watch his own interests, how much wood they burned, and how much meat they were putting down to roast. He was rich, yes, but he knew what it cost to get property together, and he quarreled all day long with his wife, who had no end of vanities in her head, now that she played the lady, and had taken to complaining of the smoke from the firewood and the nasty smell of onions.

"I want to gather my dowry together with my own hands," retorted Lucia. "My mother's daughter wants to remain an honest girl, in case any Christian should ask her to be his wife."

"Remain it then!" replied her master. "You'll see what a grand dowry it will be, and how many men will come after your honesty!"

If the macaroni was a little overcooked, if Lucia brought to table a couple of fried eggs that smelled a bit singed, Don Venerando abused her thoroughly, quite another man in his wife's presence, with his stomach stuck out and his voice loud. Did they think they were making swill for the pigs? With two servants in the kitchen sending everything to rack and ruin! Another time he'd throw the dish in her face! The mistress, blessed dear, didn't want all that racket, because of the neighbors, and she sent away the servant, squealing in falsetto: "Be off into the kitchen; get out of here, you jackanapes! You wastrel!"

Lucia went to cry her eyes out in the corner by the oven, but Brasi consoled her, with that tricky face of his.

"What does it matter? Let them rattle! If we took any notice of the masters it would be poor us! The eggs smelled burned? All the worse for them! I can't split the wood in the yard and turn the eggs at the same time. They make me do the cooking and the outside work as well, and then they expect to be waited on like the king. I should think they've forgotten the days when he used to eat bread and onion under an olive tree, and she used to go gleaning corn."

Then maidservant and cook discussed their "misfortunes," born as they were of "respectable people," and their parents were richer than the master, once upon a time. Brasi's father was a cart builder, no less, and it was the son's own fault if he hadn't wanted to follow the same trade, but had taken it into his head to go wandering around the fairs, following the cart of the travelling draper, and it was then he had learnt to cook and look after a horse and cattle.

Lucia recommenced the litany of her woes—her father, the cattle, Redhead, the bad harvest—both of them alike, she and Brasi, in that kitchen; they seemed made for each other.

"What, another case of your brother and Redhead?" replied Brasi. "Much obliged!" However he did not want to insult her with it, straight to her face. He didn't care a rap that she was a peasant. He didn't reject her out of pride. But they were both of them poor, and it would have been better to throw themselves down the well with a stone around their necks.

Lucia swallowed that bitter pill without saying a word, and if she wanted to cry she went and hid in the stair cupboard, or in the oven corner, when Brasi wasn't there. For she was now very fond of that Christian, what with being with him in front of the fire all day long. The reprimands and abuse of the master she took upon herself, and kept the best plate of food for him, and the fullest glass of wine, and went into the yard to chop wood for him, and had learned to turn the eggs and dish up the macaroni to a nicety. Brasi, as he saw her crossing herself, with her bowl on her knees, before she began to eat, said to her: "Have you never seen food in your life before?"

He grumbled at everything all the time; that it was a galley slave's life, and that he had only three hours an evening to go for a walk or to go to the inn. Lucia sometimes went so far as to ask him, with her head bent and her face growing red: "Why do you go to the inn? Leave the inn alone, it's not the place for you."

"Anybody can see you're a peasant," he replied. "You folks think there's the devil in the public house. I was born of shop workers, masters of their trade, my dear. I am not a clodhopper!"

"I say it for your good. You spend all your money, and besides there's always a chance of you starting a quarrel with somebody."

Brasi felt himself soften at these words, and at those eyes which avoided looking at him. And he allowed himself the gratification of asking:

"Well, does it matter to you, anyhow?"

"No, it doesn't matter to me. I speak for your own sake."

"Well, doesn't it get on your nerves, stooping here in the house all day long?"

"No, I thank the Lord I am so well off, and I wish all my own people were like me, and lacked for nothing."

She was just drawing the wine, squatting with the jug between her knees, and Brasi had come down into the cellar with her to show her a light. As the cellar was big and dark as a church, and not even a fly was to be heard in that subterranean place, only they two alone, Brasi and Lucia, he put his arm around her neck and kissed her on her coral-red mouth.

The poor lass remained overcome, as she crouched with her eyes on the jug, and they were both silent, she hearing his heavy breathing, and the gurgling of the wine. But then she gave a stifled cry, drawing back all trembling, so that a little of the red froth was spilled on the floor.

"Why what's amiss?" exclaimed Brasi. "As if I'd given you a slap on the face! It isn't true then that you like me?"

She dared not look him in the face, though she was dying to. She stared at the spilled wine, embarrassed, stammering:

"Oh poor me! Oh poor me! What have I done? The master's wine!"

"Eh! Let it go; he's got plenty, the master has! Listen to me rather. Don't you care for me? Say it, yes or no!"

This time she let him take her hand, without replying, and when Brasi asked her to give him the kiss back again, she gave it him, red with something that was not altogether shame.

"Have you never had one before?" asked Brasi laughing. "What a joke! You are all trembling, as if I'd said I was going to kill you."

"Yes, I do like you," she replied, "but I could hardly tell you. Don't take any notice if I'm trembling. It's because I was frightened about the wine."

"There now, think of that! You do, eh? Since when? Why didn't you tell me?"

"Since that saying we were made for one another."

"Ah!" said Brasi, scratching his head. "Let's go up, the master might come."

Lucia was all happiness since that kiss, it seemed to her as if Brasi had sealed on her mouth his promise to marry her. But he never spoke of it, and if the girl tried him on that score, he replied: "What are you bothering about? Besides, what's the good putting our necks in the yoke, when we can be together just as if we were married."

"No, it's not the same. Now you fend for yourself and I fend for myself, but when we are married, we shall be one."

"And a lovely thing that will be, an' all! Besides, we don't belong to the same walk of life. It would be different if you had a bit of dowry."

"Ah! What a black heart you've got! No! You've never cared for me!"

"Yes, I have! And I'm ready for you for whatever you want of me; but without talking about that there—"

"No! I don't want any of that sort of thing! Leave me alone, and don't look at me anymore!"

Now, she knew what men were like. All liars and traitors. She didn't want to hear of it anymore. She'd rather throw herself headfirst down the well; she wanted to become a Daughter of Mary; she wanted to take her good name and throw it out the window! What good was it to her, without a dowry? She wanted to break her neck with that old creature her master, and get her dowry out of her shame. Don Venerando was always hanging round her, first saying nice things and then nasty, looking after his own interests, seeing if they put too much wood on the fire, how much oil they used for the frying, sending Brasi to buy a half a penny's worth of snuff, and trying to take Lucia by the chin, running around after her in the kitchen, on tiptoe so his wife shouldn't hear, scolding the girl for her lack of respect for him, making him run in that fashion! "No! No!" She was like a mad cat. She'd rather take her things and go! "And where shall you find anything to eat? And how shall you find a husband, without a dowry? Look at these earrings! Then I'll give you fifty notes for your dowry. Brasi would have both his eyes pulled out, for fifty notes."

Ah, that black-hearted Brasi! He left her in the wicked hands of her master, which trembled as they pawed at her. Left her with the thought of her mother, who hadn't long to live; and of the bare house empty of everything except trouble, and of Pino the Tome who had thrown her over to go and eat the bread of the widow! He left her with the temptation of the earrings and the fifty notes in her head!

And one day she came into the kitchen with her face all dismayed, and the gold pendants dangling against her cheeks. Brasi opened his eyes, and said to her; "How fine you look now, Neighbor Lucia!"

"Ah! You like me in them? All right, all right!"

Brasi, now that he saw the earrings and the rest, strove so hard to show himself helpful and useful to her, that you might have thought she had become another mistress in the house. He left her the fuller plate, and the best seat at the fire. And he opened his heart wide to her, that they were two poor things both of them, and it did your soul good to tell your troubles to somebody you were fond of. And as soon as he could scrape fifty notes together he'd set up a little public house and take a wife. He in the kitchen, she behind the bar. And then you weren't at anybody's bidding. If the master liked to do them a good turn, he could do it without hurting himself, because fifty notes was a pinch of snuff to him. And Brasi wouldn't look down his nose, not him! One hand washes the other in this world. And it wasn't his fault if he tried to earn his living as best he could. Poverty wasn't a sin.

But Lucia went red-and-white, her eyes swelled with tears, or she hid her face in her apron. After some time she didn't show herself outside the house, neither for Mass, nor for confession, nor at Easter, nor at Christmas. In the kitchen she hid herself in the darkest corner, with her face dropped, huddled in the new dress her master had given her, wide around the waist.

Brasi consoled her with kind words. He put his arm round her neck, felt the fine stuff of her frock, and praised it. Those gold earrings were made for her. Anybody who is well dressed and has money in her pocket has no need to feel ashamed and walk with her eyes down; above all when the eyes are as lovely as Neighbor Lucia's. The poor thing took courage by looking into his face with those same eyes, still overcome, and she stammered: "Do you mean it, Master Brasi? Do you still care for me?"

"Yes, yes, I do really!" replied Brasi, with his hand on his conscience. "But is it my fault if I'm not rich enough to marry you? If you'd got fifty notes, I'd marry you with my eyes shut."

Don Venerando had now taken to liking him also, and gave him his old clothes and his broken boots. When he went down into the cellar he gave him a good pot of wine, saying to him:

"Here, drink my health!"

And his fat belly shook with laughing, seeing the grimaces which Brasi made, and hearing him stuttering to Lucia, pale as a dead man: "The master is a gentleman, Neighbor Lucia! Let the neighbors cackle, they're all jealous, because they're dying with hunger, and they'd like to be in your shoes."

Santo, the brother, heard the gossip in the square some month or so later. He ran to his wife, staggered. Poor they had always been, but honorable. Red-head was also overwhelmed, and she ran in dismay to her sister-in-law, who couldn't utter a word. But when she came back home, she was quite different, serene and with roses in her cheeks.

"If you did but see! A chest as high as this, full of white goods! And rings, and pendant earrings, and necklaces of fine gold. Then there are fifty notes for the dowry. A real God's provision!"

"And what by that?" the brother kept saying from time to time, unable to take it all in. "At least she might have waited till our mother had closed her eyes!"

All this took place in the year of the snow, when a good many roofs fell in, and there was a great mortality among the cattle of the district, God preserve us!

At Lamia and on the Mount of Santa Margherita, as folks saw that livid evening declining, heavy with ill-omened clouds, so that the oxen looked suspiciously behind them, and mooed, all the people stood outside their huts to gaze far off toward the sea, with one hand over their eyes, not speaking. The bell of the Old Monastery, at the top of the village, was ringing to drive away the bad night, and on the Castle hillcrest there was a great swarming of goodwives, seen black against the pale sky rim, watching the Dragon's Tail in the sky, a pitch-black stripe that smelled of sulfur, they said, and which meant it was going to be a bad night. The women made signs with their fingers to conjure him away, the dragon, and they showed him the little medal of the Madonna on their bare breasts, and spat in his face, making the sign of the cross upon themselves right down to their navels, and praying God and the souls in purgatory, and Santa Lucia, whose eve it was, to protect their fields, their cattle, and also their men, all living creatures that were outside the village. At the beginning of winter Carmenio had gone with the flock to Santa

Margherita. His mother wasn't well that evening, and tossed in her bed, with her dilated eyes, and wouldn't keep quiet like she usually did, but wanted this, and wanted that, and wanted to get up, and wanted them to turn her over onto the other side. Carmenio had run around for a while, attending to her, trying to do something. Then he had posted himself by the bed, stupefied, with his hands clutching his hair.

The hut was across the stream, in the bed of the valley, between two great rocks which leaned over the roof. Opposite, the coast, seeming to stand on end, was beginning to fade in the darkness which was rising from the valley, naked and black with stones, and between the stones the white stripe of the road lost itself. When the sun was setting the neighbors had come from the flock in the cactus grove, to see if the sick woman wanted anything; but she was lying quite still in her bit of a bed, with her face upward and her nose going black, as if dusted with soot.

"A bad sign!" Herdsman Decu had said. "If I hadn't got the sheep up above, and the bad weather that's coming on, I wouldn't leave you alone tonight. Call me, if there's anything!"

Carmenio said yes, with his head leaning against the doorpost; but seeing him going away step by step, to be lost in the night, he had a great desire to run after him, to begin to shout, and tear his hair—to do he knew not what.

"If anything happens," shouted Herdsman Decu from the distance, "run up to the flock in the cactus thicket, up there, there's people there."

The flock was still to be seen on the rocky height, skywards, in that dim of twilight which still gathered on the tops of the mountains, and penetrated the thickets of the cactus. Far, far away, toward Lamia and the plain, was heard the howling of dogs—*waow! waow! waow!*—the sound coming right up to there and making your bones turn cold.

Then the sheep suddenly were possessed and began to rush about in a mass in the enclosure, driven by a mad terror, as if they heard the wolf in the neighborhood; and at that frantic clanging of sheep bells, it seemed as if the shadows had become lit up with so many fiery eyes, all going around. Then the sheep stopped still, huddled close together, with their noses down to the ground, and the dog with one long and lamentable howl, left off barking, seated there on his tail.

"If I'd known," thought Carmenio, "it would have been better to tell Herdsman Decu not to leave me alone."

Outside, in the darkness, the bells of the flock were heard shuddering from time to time. Through the window you could see the square of the black doorway, black as the mouth of an oven; nothing else. And the coast away opposite and the deep valley and the plain of Lamia, all was plunged in that bottomless blackness, so that it seemed as if what you saw was nothing but the noise of the torrent, away below, mounting up toward the hut, swollen and threatening.

If he had known this, too, he'd have run to the village before it got dark, to fetch his brother; and then of course by this time he'd have been there with him, and Lucia as well, and the sister-in-law.

Then the mother began to speak, but you couldn't make out what she said, and she kept grasping the bedclothes with her wasted hands.

"Mamma! Mamma! What do you want?" asked Carmenio. "Tell me what it is, I'm here with you!"

But the mother did not answer. She shook her head instead, as if to say no! No! She didn't want to. The boy put the candle under her nose and burst out crying with fear.

"Oh, Mamma! Oh, Mamma!" whimpered Carmenio. "Oh, I'm all alone and I can't help you!" He opened the door to call the folks from the flock among the cactus. But nobody heard him. Everywhere there was a dense glimmer; on the coast, in the valley, and down on the plain—like a silence made of cotton wool. All at once came the sound of a muffled bell from far off—'*nton! nton! nton!* — and it seemed to curdle in the snow.

"Oh, holiest Madonna!" sobbed Carmenio. "Whatever bell is that? Oh, you with the cactus sheep, help! Help! Holy Christians!" he began to shout.

At last, above there, at the top of the cactus hill, was heard a far-off voice, like the bell of Francoforte.

"Ooooh! … what's the … m-a-a-a-t-t-e-r? What's the maaatter?"

"Help, good Christians! Help, here at Shepherd Decu-u-u's—"

"Ooooh!—follow the shee-eeep!—fo-o-ollow!"

"No! no! it isn't the sheep—it isn't!"

Just then the screech-owl flew past and began to screech over the hut.

"There!" murmured Carmenio, crossing himself. "Now the screech owl has smelled the smell of dead people. Now my mamma is going to die!"

Having to stay alone in the cabin with his mother, who no longer spoke, made him want to cry. "Mamma, what's the matter? Mamma, tell me! Mamma, are you cold?" She did not breathe, her face was dark. He lit the fire between the two stones of the hearth, and sat watching how the boughs burned, how they made a flame and then breathed out as if they were saying something about it.

When he had been with the flocks at Resecone, the Francoforte man, as they sat up at night, had told tales of witches who ride on broomsticks, and do witchcraft over the flames of the hearth. Carmenio remembered even now how the farm people had gathered to listen, with all their eyes open, in front of the little light hung to the pillar of the great dark millstone, and that not one of them had had the courage afterward to go and sleep in his own corner that evening.

Against these things he had the medal of the Madonna under his shirt, and the ribbon of Santa Agrippina tied round his wrist, till it had become black with wear. And in his pocket he had the reed whistle, which reminded him of summer evenings—*Yoo! Yoo!*—when they let the sheep into the stubble that is yellow as gold, and the grasshoppers explode in sound at the hour of noon, and the larks fall whistling to nestle behind the sods at sunset, when the scent of wild mint and marjoram wakes up. *Yoo! Yoo!* Infant Jesus! At Christmas, when he had gone to the village, that was how they had played for the novena in front of the little altar that was lit up and adorned with boughs of orange tree; and in front of the doors of all the houses the children had been tossing stones, the fine December sun shining on their backs. Then they had all set off for the midnight Mass, in a crowd with the neighbors, colliding and laughing through the dark streets. Ah, why had he got this thorn in his heart now? And why didn't his mother say anything! It was still a long time till midnight. Between the stones of the unplastered walls it seemed as if there were eyes watching from every hole, looking into the hut, at the hearth, eyes black and frozen.

On a straw stack in a corner a jacket was thrown down, spread out long, and it seemed as if the sleeves were swelling out; and the devil with the Archangel Michael, in the image stuck on to the headboard, gnashed his white teeth, with his hands in his hair, among the red zigzags of hell.

Next day, pale as so many corpses, arrived Santo, and Redhead with the children trailing after her, and Lucia who had no thought for concealing her condition, in that hour of anguish. Around the bed of the dead woman they tore their hair and beat their heads, and thought of nothing else. Then as Santo noticed his sister with so much stomach on her that it was shameful, he began saying in the midst of all the blubbering: "You might at least have let that poor woman close her eyes first, you might—"

And Lucia on her side:

"If I'd only known, if I'd only known! She shouldn't have gone short of doctor or druggist, now I've got fifty dollars of my own."

"She is in Paradise praying to God for us sinners," concluded Redhead. "She knows you've got your dowry and she's at peace, poor thing. Now Master Brasi will marry you without fail."

1882

THE FIFTH STORY
DAY THE SEVENTH

Giovanni Boccaccio

A JEALOUS HUSBAND, IN THE GUISE OF A PRIEST,
CONFESSETH HIS WIFE, WHO GIVETH HIM TO BELIEVE
THAT SHE LOVETH A PRIEST, WHO COMETH TO HER EVERY
NIGHT; AND WHILST THE HUSBAND SECRETLY KEEPETH
WATCH AT THE DOOR FOR THE LATTER, THE LADY BRINGETH
IN A LOVER OF HERS BY THE ROOF AND LIETH WITH HIM

Lauretta having made an end of her story and all having commended the lady for that she had done aright and even as befitted her wretch of a husband, the king, to lose no time, turned to Fiammetta and courteously imposed on her the burden of the story-telling; whereupon she began thus: Most noble ladies, the foregoing story moveth me to tell you, likewise, of a jealous husband, accounting, as I do, all that their wives do unto such,— particularly when they are jealous without cause,—to be well done and holding that, if the makers of the laws had considered everything, they should have appoint-ed no other penalty unto women who offend in this than that which they appoint unto whoso offendeth against other in self-defense; for that jealous men are plotters against the lives of young women and most diligent pro-curers of their deaths. Wives abide all the week mewed up at home, occupy-ing themselves with domestic offices and the occasions of their families and households, and after they would fain, like every one else, have some solace and some rest on holidays and be at leisure to take some diversion even as do the tillers of the fields, the artisans of the towns and the administrators of the laws, according to the example of God himself, who rested from all His labors the seventh day, and to the intent of the laws, both human and Divine, which, looking to the honor of God and the common weal of all, have distinguished working days from those of repose. But to this jealous men will on no wise consent; nay, those days which are gladsome for all oth-er women they make wretcheder and more doleful than the others to their wives, keeping them yet closelier straitened and confined; and what a mis-ery and a languishment this is for the poor creatures those only know who have proved it. Wherefore, to conclude, I say that what a woman doth to a husband who is jealous without cause should certainly not be condemned, but rather commended.

There was, then, in Arimino a merchant, very rich both in lands and monies, who, having to wife a very fair lady, became beyond measure jealous of her; nor had he other cause for this save that, as he loved her exceedingly and held her very fair and saw that she studied with all her might to please him, even so he imagined that every man loved her and that she appeared fair to all and eke that she studied to please others as she did himself, which was the reasoning of a man of nought and one of little sense. Being grown thus jealous, he kept such strict watch over her and held her in such constraint that belike many there be of those who are condemned to capital punish-ment who are less straitly guarded of their gaolers; for, far from being at liberty to go to weddings or entertainments or to church or indeed anywise to set foot without the house, she dared not even stand at the window nor look abroad on any occasion; wherefore her life was most wretched and she brooked this annoy with the more impatience as she felt herself the less to blame. Accordingly, seeing herself unjustly suspected of her husband, she determined, for her own solace, to find a means (if she but might) of doing on such wise that he should have reason for his ill usage of her. And for that she might not station herself at the window and so had no opportunity of showing herself favorable to the suit of any one who might take note of her, as he passed along her street, and pay his court to her, knowing that in the adjoining house there was a certain young man both handsome and agreeable, she bethought herself to look if there were any hole in the wall that parted the two houses and through which to spy once and again till such time as she should see the youth aforesaid and find an occasion of speaking with him and bestowing on him her love, so he would accept thereof, purposing, if a means could be found, to foregather with him bytimes and on this wise while away her sorry life till such time as the demon [of jealousy] should take leave of her husband.

Accordingly, she went spying about the walls of the house, now in one part and now in another, whenas her husband was abroad, and happened at last upon a very privy place where the wall was somewhat opened by a fissure and looking therethrough, albeit she could ill discover what was on the other side, yet she perceived that the opening gave upon a bedchamber there and said in herself, "Should this be the chamber of Filippo," to wit, the youth her neighbor, "I were half sped." Then, causing secretly enquire of this by a maid of hers, who had pity upon her, she found that the young man did indeed sleep in that chamber all alone; wherefore, by dint of often visiting the crevice and dropping pebbles and such small matters, whenas she perceived him to be there, she wrought on such wise that he came to the opening, to see what was to do; whereupon she called to him softly. He, knowing her voice, answered her, and she, profiting by the occasion, discovered to him in brief all her mind; whereat the youth was mightily content and made shift to enlarge the hole from his side on such wise that none could perceive it; and therethrough they many a time bespoke one another and touched hands, but could go no farther, for the jealous vigilance of the husband.

After awhile, the Feast of the Nativity drawing near, the lady told her husband that, an it pleased him, she would fain go to church on Christmas morning and confess and take the sacrament, as other Christians did. Quoth he, "And what sin hast thou committed that thou wouldst confess?" "How?" answered the lady. "Thinkest thou that I am a saint, because thou keepest me mewed up? Thou must know well enough that I commit sins like all others that live in this world; but I will not tell them to thee, for that thou art not a priest." The jealous wretch took suspicion at these words and determined to seek to know what sins she had committed; wherefore, having bethought himself of a means whereby he might gain his end, he answered that he was content, but that he would have her go to no other church than their parish chapel and that thither she must go betimes in the morning and confess herself either to their chaplain or to such priest as the latter should appoint her and to none other and presently return home. Herseemed she half apprehended his meaning; but without saying otherwhat, she answered that she would do as he said.

Accordingly, Christmas Day come, the lady arose at daybreak and attiring herself, repaired to the church appointed her of her husband, who, on his part, betook himself to the same place and reached it before her. Having already taken order with the chaplain of that which he had a mind to do, he hastily donned one of the latter's gowns, with a great flapped cowl, such as we see priests wear, and drawing the hood a little over his face, seated himself in the choir. The lady, entering the chapel, enquired for the chaplain, who came and hearing from her that she would fain confess, said that he could not hear her, but would send her one of his brethren. Accordingly, going away, he sent her the jealous man, in an ill hour for the latter, who came up with a very grave air, and albeit the day was not over bright and he had drawn the cowl far over his eyes, knew not so well to disguise himself but he was readily recognized by the lady, who, seeing this, said in herself, "Praised be God! From a jealous man he is turned priest; but no matter; I will e'en give him what he goeth seeking."

Accordingly, feigning not to know him, she seated herself at his feet. My lord Jealousy had put some pebbles in his mouth, to impede his speech somewhat, so his wife might not know him by his voice, himseeming he was in every other particular so thoroughly disguised that he was nowise fearful of being recognized by her. To come to the confession, the lady told him, amongst other things, (having first declared herself to be married,) that she was enamored of a priest, who came every night to lie with her. When the jealous man heard this, himseemed he had gotten a knife-thrust in the heart, and had not desire constrained him to know more, he had abandoned the confession and gone away. Standing fast, then, he asked the lady, "How! Doth not your husband lie with you?" "Ay doth he, sir," replied she. "How, then," asked the jealous man, "can the priest also lie with you?" "Sir," answered she, "by what art he doth it I know not, but there is not a door in the house so fast locked but it openeth so soon as he toucheth it; and he telleth me that, whenas he cometh to the door of my chamber, before opening it, he pronounceth certain words, by virtue whereof my husband incontinent falleth asleep, and so soon as he perceiveth him to be fast, he openeth the door and cometh in and lieth with me; and this never faileth." Quoth the mock priest, "Madam, this is ill done, and it behoveth you altogether to refrain therefrom." "Sir," answered the lady, "methinketh I could never do that, for that I love him too well." "Then," said the other, "I cannot shrive you." Quoth she, "I am grieved for that; but I came not hither to tell you lies; if I thought I could do it, I would tell you so." "In truth, madam," replied the husband, "I am concerned for you, for that I see you lose your soul at this game; but, to do you service, I will well to take the pains of putting up my special orisons to God in your name, the which maybe shall profit you, and I will send you bytimes a little clerk of mine, to whom you shall say if they have profited you or not; and if they have profited you, we will proceed farther." "Sir," answered the lady, "whatever you do, send none to me at home, for, should my husband come to know of it, he is so terribly jealous that nothing in the world would get it out of his head that your messenger came hither for nothing but ill, and I should have no peace with him this year to come." Quoth the other, "Madam, have no fear of that, for I will certainly contrive it on such wise that you shall never hear a word of the matter from him." Then said she, "So but you can engage to do that, I am content." Then, having made her confession and gotten her penance, she rose to her feet and went off to hear Mass; whilst the jealous man, (ill luck go with him!) withdrew, bursting with rage, to put off his priest's habit, and returned home, impatient to find a means of surprising the priest with his wife, so he might play the one and the other an ill turn.

Presently the lady came back from church and saw plainly enough from her husband's looks that she had given him an ill Christmas; albeit he studied, as most he might, to conceal that which he had done and what himseemed he had learned. Then, being inwardly resolved to lie in wait near the street-door that night and watch for the priest's coming, he said to the lady, "Needs must I sup and lie abroad tonight, wherefore look thou lock the street-door fast, as well as that of the midstair and that of thy chamber, and get thee to bed, whenas it seemeth good to thee." The lady answered, "It is well," and betaking herself, as soon as she had leisure, to the hole in the wall, she made the wonted signal, which when Filippo heard, he came to her forthright. She told him how she had done that morning and what her husband had said to her after dinner and added, "I am certain he will not leave the house, but will set himself to watch the door; wherefore do thou find means to come hither to me tonight by the roof, so we may lie together." The young man was mightily rejoiced at this and answered, "Madam, leave me do."

Accordingly, the night come, the jealous man took his arms and hid himself by stealth in a room on the ground floor, whilst the lady, whenas it seemed to her time, having caused lock all the doors and in particular that of the midstair, so he might not avail to come up, summoned the young man, who came to her from his side by a very privy way. Thereupon they went to bed and gave themselves a good time, taking their pleasure one of the other till daybreak, when the young man returned to his own house. Meanwhile, the jealous man stood to his arms well nigh all night beside the street-door, sorry and supperless and dying of cold, and waited for the priest to come till near upon day, when, unable to watch any longer, he returned to the ground floor room and there fell asleep. Towards tierce he awoke and the street-door being now open, he made a show of returning from otherwhere and went up into his house and dined. A little after, he sent a lad, as he were the priest's clerkling that had confessed her, to the lady to ask if she wot of were come thither again. She knew the messenger well enough and answered that he had not come thither that night and that if he did thus, he might haply pass out of her mind, albeit she wished it not. What more should I tell you? The jealous man abode on the watch night after night, looking to catch the priest at his entering in, and the lady still had a merry life with her lover the while.

At length the cuckold, able to contain himself no longer, asked his wife, with an angry air, what she had said to the priest the morning she had confessed herself to him. She answered that she would not tell him, for that it was neither a just thing nor a seemly; whereupon, "Vile woman that thou art!" cried he. "In despite of thee I know what thou saidst to him, and needs must I know the priest of whom thou art so mightily enamored and who, by means of his conjurations, lieth with thee every night; else will I slit thy weasand." She replied that it was not true that she was enamored of any priest. "How?" cried the husband, "Saidst thou not thus and thus to the priest who confessed thee?" And she, "Thou couldst not have reported it better, not to say if he had told it thee, but if thou hadst been present; ay, I did tell him this." "Then," rejoined the jealous man, "tell me who is this priest, and that quickly."

The lady fell a-smiling and answered, "It rejoiceth me mightily to see a wise man led by the nose by a woman, even as one leadeth a ram by the horns to the shambles, albeit thou art no longer wise nor hast been since the hour when, unknowing why, thou sufferedst the malignant spirit of jealousy to enter thy breast; and the sillier and more besotted thou art, so much the less is my glory thereof. Deemest thou, husband mine, I am as blind of the eyes of the body as thou of those of the mind? Certainly, no; I perceived at first sight who was the priest that confessed me and know that thou wast he; but I had it at heart to give thee that which thou wentest seeking, and in sooth I have done it. Wert thou as wise as thou thinkest to be, thou wouldst not have essayed by this means to learn the secrets of thy good wife, but wouldst, without taking vain suspicion, have recognized that which she confessed to thee to be the very truth, without her having sinned in aught. I told thee that I loved a priest, and wast not thou, whom I am much to blame to love as I do, become a priest? I told thee that no door of my house could abide locked, whenas he had a mind to lie with me; and what door in the house was ever kept against thee, whenas thou wouldst come whereas I might be? I told thee that the priest lay with me every night, and when was it that thou layest not with me? And whenassoever thou sentest thy clerk to me, which was thou knowest, as often as thou layest from me, I sent thee word that the priest had not been with me. What other than a crack-brain like thee, who has suffered thyself to be blinded by thy jealousy, had failed to understand these things? Thou hast abidden in the house, keeping watch anights, and thoughtest to have given me to believe that thou wast gone abroad to sup and sleep. Bethink thee henceforth and become a man again, as thou wast wont to be; and make not thyself a laughing stock to whoso knoweth thy fashions, as do I, and leave this unconscionable watching that thou keepest; for I swear to God that, if the fancy took me to make thee wear the horns, I would engage, haddest thou an hundred eyes, as thou hast but two, to do my pleasure on such wise that thou shouldst not be ware thereof."

The jealous wretch, who thought to have very adroitly surprised his wife's secrets, hearing this, avouched himself befooled and without answering otherwhat, held the lady for virtuous and discreet; and whenas it behooved him to be jealous, he altogether divested himself of his jealousy, even as he had put it on, what time he had no need thereof. Wherefore the discreet lady, being in a manner licensed to do her pleasures, thenceforward no longer caused her lover to come to her by the roof, as go the cats, but e'en brought him in at the door, and dealing advisedly, many a day thereafter gave herself a good time and led a merry life with him.

1351

TO THE TENTH MUSE

Matilde Serao

"NOËL, NOËL! JOY, JOY!"

Up above: a calm and quiet little room, with a sweetly warm ambience. A lamp pours its even, restful light over the pages of a good book; here and there a smile of friendship, or of love—the hours pass slowly and placidly, like lovely, languid people. Down below: the wet and muddy street, slippery with mire, is trampled by thousands of feet; a thick fog made of smoke, dampness, warm scirocco air, people's breath; the darkness violently pierced by gaslights, smoking oil lamps, the reddish light of torches, the vivid colors of holiday fireworks; the comings, goings, encounters, and cries of a crowd that is dense, constant, ever-changing, and that talks, laughs, shouts, makes a din, sings, and yells; a clamor that courses the whole range of pitch from the highest to the lowest tones, with the wildest shifts from an extremely high-pitched racket to a deep thunderclap. Although the shutters are closed and the double walls are lined, echoes of that uproar make their way to the reader;

distracted, he listens and smiles. The room's temperature is pleasant, the carpet is soft, the light is soothing, the book displays the appeal of its pale yellow paper, its tapered lettering, its whimsical ornaments and verses; but all in vain; the great voice of the crowd is insistent, rising and resounding like a powerful summons. Then the reader is possessed by nostalgia for the street, the fog, the hustle and bustle; he feels a sharp desire to go down into that tumult, to enjoy that scene, to contribute his part to it, to feel small, insignificant, and lost in it; he no longer fights against this desire, but yields to it; and with an enormous sigh, the street triumphs over the little room.

All the riches of the vegetable and animal kingdoms lie jumbled in profusion in the squares and streets. Here is the triumph of meat: there are rows of chickens hung by the legs, with their yellowish, firm skin lightly dotted with brown and veined with pale light blue; there are turkeys, fat and round, swinging somberly in the scirocco with the same seriousness as if they were still alive. The flickering torchlight puts into strange profile enormous heaps of veal, whose whitish flesh is bloody, with long, strong muscle fibers and smooth, polished, unblemished bones; and fully illuminates the white suckling pigs, with their almost elegant figures, which are the tender, juicy, and preferred meal of fine ladies and priests. You walk forever and see only meat—and then that smell of freshly slaughtered animals, that dripping reddish-brown blood, those sharp and decisive knife strokes, lead you to feel melancholy and disgust: the triumph of full, fat, heavy, insolent matter, smiling at its own death that is a new life, and at once provocative and sickening, ends up crushing you. With a sense of fear, you think of that luxury, that excess, that exuberance, that enormity—and anxiously you seek out milder sensations.

Next there come into view herbs, greens, fruits: a veritable vegetable sweetness, the tribute of the countryside, the offering of the fields and forests. The little mounds of green broccoli, whose florets look like pointed lace work, gaze with disdain at the humble little chicory, harvested in small bunches, on which droplets of water are shining; the large, tightly closed white cabbages seem to want to burst from their wrapper of light green leaves, while the black cabbages blend with the darkness, almost as if seeking solitude. The rippling light when people or carriages pass by, a sudden burst of fireworks, a supervening shadow; all these contribute to the fantastic nature of this scene. Proportions seem to grow in size, you lose your sense of reality and seem to be walking in fields of marjoram and clover, between two hedges made of vegetables, while at the end, as a horizon, the yellow flame of a pyramid of oranges is lit, like a souvenir of Sicilian sunsets. The sharp, sometimes inebriating scent of apples reaches your brain; there is also the sweeter and seemingly older scent of pears brought out of winter storage, and the subtle, light, and exhilarating effluvium of mandarins. But a stronger and healthier smell drives away all the others, replacing them and becoming the sole ruler.

You now enter the domain of the sea; in small, fringed, seaweed baskets, looking like the loose hair of a beautiful dead water-nymph, eels with brown backs and pale bellies quiver, writhe, and twist themselves in knots, while lobsters, usually so calm and resigned, agitate their long pointed legs. Pink mullets move their fins a little in order to breathe, oysters open their shells ever so slightly, and razor clams known as *cannolicchi* (in Naples, *soleni*) slip out of their long cases, almost as if seeking freedom. Codfish have died in a desperate position, their bodies half twisted with tails raised, almost as if they had suffered a slow and painful end; other more dignified fish, convinced of their fate, stayed still and proud. There is nonstop spraying of seawater, and loud, robust cries coming from the chests of men who have battled gales; these are sinewy, swarthy fishermen with bare legs and arms, who are happy to offer you their wares. The sea—the good old sea, that beneficent curmudgeon, that lavish eternal grumbler—very willingly gave up a little of its wealth, and left its grandiose calling card, in this colossal display. Let's have a smile and recall playful summer swims, the coolness of the waves, and rocks crowned with seafoam!

But the glow of gaslight—refracted in shiny faceted crystals, in gilded ornaments, in silver sequins, in brightly colored satins—draws your gaze to a store window, or two or three. Here are the sweets, with light, graceful, simple forms resembling flowers, fruit, hearts, and butterflies; with delicate, soft colors, such as translucent pink, opalescent green, grayish white, and pale violet, all of which melt together and blend into a palette of pastels pleasing to the eye. There are soft, fluffy foams looking as though they might vanish if a single puff of air were to touch them; wobbling creams, either white or yellow; candied fruit, covered with a silvery transparent film, in shiny cascades; the solemn weightiness of nougats, and dark brown chocolate in all its forms and aspects; light puff pastries that dissolve when you bite into them; dates stuffed with pistachios in a most noble union, like that of milk and honey. It is, in short, the gathering of all that is finest, most tender and elegant; these are caresses for the senses of sight, taste, and smell; in these sweets, refinement and deliciousness are given their most complete embodiment. We may find here the culmination of every desire, no matter how extraordinary; the highest and purest poetry of human sensations; fantasy that has been brought to life; the artistic ideal made real; the sum of art itself.

With this sublime lyric flight concludes the splendid hymn that the people of Naples have dedicated to the tenth muse: Gasterea.[1]

Christmas 1878

---

1 Jean Anthelme Brillat-Savarin, *The Physiology of Taste, or, Meditations on Transcendental Gastronomy* (New York: Courier Dover Publications, 2002 [1925]), 244: "Gasterea is the Tenth Muse: the delights of taste are her domain. The empire of the world were hers, would she but claim it; for the world is nothing without life, and all that lives takes nourishment." Brillat-Savarin's influential work was first published in Paris in 1825, and was well known in late nineteenth-century Italy.

WINTER IN THE ABRUZZI

Natalia Ginzburg

GOD HAS GIVEN US THIS MOMENT OF PEACE.

There are only two seasons in the Abruzzi: summer and winter. The spring is snowy and windy like the winter, and the autumn is hot and clear like the summer. Summer starts in June and ends in November. The long days of sunshine on the low, parched hills, the yellow dust in the streets and the babies' dysentery come to an end, and winter begins. People stop living in the streets: the barefoot children disappear from the church steps. In the region I am talking about almost all the men disappeared after the last crops were brought in: they went for work to Terni, Sulmona or Rome. Many bricklayers came from that area, and some of the houses were elegantly built; they were like small villas with terraces and little columns, and when you entered them you would be astonished to find large dark kitchens with hams hanging from the ceilings, and vast, dirty, empty rooms. In the kitchen a fire would be burning, and there were various kinds of fire: there were great fires of oak logs, fires of branches and leaves, fires of twigs picked up one by one in the street. It was easier to tell the rich from the poor by looking at the fires they burned than by looking at the houses or at the people themselves, or at their clothes and shoes which were all more or less the same.

When I first arrived in that countryside all the faces looked the same to me, all the women—rich and poor, young and old—resembled one another. Almost all of them had toothless mouths: exhaustion and a wretched diet, the unremitting overwork of childbirth and breast feeding, mean that women lose their teeth there when they are thirty. But then, gradually, I began to distinguish Vincenzina from Secondina, Annunziata from Addolerata, and I began to go into their houses and warm myself at their various fires.

When the first snows began to fall a quiet sadness took hold of us. We were in exile: our city was a long way off, and so were books, friends, the various desultory events of a real existence. We lit our green stove with its long chimney that went through the ceiling: we gathered together in the room with the stove—there we cooked and ate, my husband wrote at the big oval table, the children covered the floor with toys. There was an eagle painted on the ceiling of the room, and I used to look at the eagle and think that was exile. Exile was the eagle, the murmur of the green stove, the vast, silent countryside and the motionless snow. At five o'clock the bell of the church of Santa Maria would ring and the women with their black shawls and red faces went to Benediction. Every evening my husband and I went for a walk: every evening we walked arm in arm, sinking our feet into the snow. The houses that ran alongside the street were lived in by people we knew and liked, and they all used to come to the door to greet us. Sometimes one would ask, "When will you go back to your own house?" My husband answered, "When the war is over." "And when will this war be over? You know everything and you're a professor, when will it be over?" They called my husband "the professor" because they could not pronounce his name, and they came from a long way off to ask his advice on the most diverse things—the best season for having teeth out, the subsidies which the town hall gave and the different taxes and duties.

In winter when an old person died of pneumonia the bell of Santa Maria sounded the death knell and Domenico Orecchia, the joiner, made the coffin. A woman went mad and they took her to the lunatic asylum at Collemaggio, and this was the talk of the countryside for a while. She was a young, clean woman, the cleanest in the whole district; they said it was excessive cleanliness that had done it to her. Girl twins were born to Gigetto di Calcedonio who already had boy twins, and there was a row at the town hall because the authorities did not want to give the family any help as they had quite a bit of land and an immense kitchen-garden. A neighbor spat in the eye of Rosa, the school caretaker, and she went about with her eye bandaged because she intended to pay back the insult. "The eye is a delicate thing, and spit is salty," she explained. And this was talked about for a while, until there was nothing else to say about it.

Every day homesickness grew in us. Sometimes it was even pleasant, like being in gentle, slightly intoxicating company. Letters used to arrive from our city with news of marriages and deaths from which we were excluded. Sometimes our homesickness was sharp and bitter, and turned into hatred; then we hated Domenico Orecchia, Gigetto di Calcedonio, Annunziatina, the bells of Santa Maria. But it was a hatred which we kept hidden because we knew it was unjust; and our house was always full of people who came to ask for favors and to offer them. Sometimes the dressmaker made a special kind of dumpling for us. She would wrap a cloth around her waist and beat the eggs, and send Crocetta around the countryside to see if she could borrow a really big saucepan. Her red face was absorbed in her work and her eyes shone with a proud determination. She would have burned the house down to make her dumplings come out a success. Her clothes and hair became white with flour and then she would place the dumplings with great care on the oval table where my husband wrote.

Crocetta was our serving woman. In fact she was not a woman because she was only fourteen years old. It was the dressmaker who had found her. The dressmaker divided the world into two groups—those who comb their hair and those who do not comb their hair. It was necessary to be on the lookout against those who do not comb their hair because, naturally, they have lice. Crocetta combed her hair; and so she came to work for us and tell our children long stories about death and cemeteries. Once upon a time there was a little boy whose mother died. His father chose another wife and this stepmother didn't love the little boy. So she killed him when his father was out in the fields, and she boiled him in a stew. His father came home for supper, but, after he had finished eating, the bones that were left on the plate started to sing:

Mummy with an angry frown
Popped me in the cooking pot,
When I was done and piping hot
Greedy daddy gulped me down.

Then the father killed his wife with a scythe and he hung her from a nail in front of the door. Sometimes I find myself murmuring the words of the song in the story, and then the whole country is in front of me again, together with the particular atmosphere of its seasons, its yellow gusting wind and the sound of its bells.

Every morning I went out with my children and there was a general amazed disapproval that I should expose them to the cold and the snow. "What sin have the poor creatures committed?" people said. "This isn't the time for walking, dear. Go back home." I went for long walks in the white deserted countryside, and the few people I met looked at the children with pity. "What sin have they committed?" they said to me. There, if a baby is born in winter they do not take it out of the room until the summer comes. At midday my husband used to catch me up with the post and we went back to the house together.

I talked to the children about our city. They had been very small when we left, and had no memories of it at all. I told them that there the houses had many stories, that there were so many houses and so many streets, and so many big fine shops. "But here there is Giro's," the children said.

Giro's shop was exactly opposite our house. Giro used to stand in the doorway like an old owl, gazing at the street with his round, indifferent eyes. He sold a bit of everything; groceries and candles, postcards, shoes and oranges. When the stock arrived and Giro unloaded the crates, boys ran to eat the rotten oranges that he threw away. At Christmas nougat, liqueurs and sweets also arrived. But he never gave the slightest discount on his prices. "How mean you are, Giro," the women said to him, and he answered "People who aren't mean get eaten by dogs." At Christmas the men returned from

Terni, Sulmona and Rome, stayed for a few days, and set off again after they had slaughtered the pigs. For a few days people ate nothing but *sfrizzoli*, incredible sausages that made you drink the whole time; and then the squeal of the new piglets would fill the street.

In February the air was soft and damp. Gray, swollen clouds traveled across the sky. One year during the thaw the gutters broke. Then water began to pour into the house and the rooms became a veritable quagmire. But it was like this throughout the whole area; not one house remained dry. The women emptied buckets out of their windows and swept the water out of their front doors. There were people who went to bed with an open umbrella. Domenico Orecchia said that it was a punishment for some sin. This lasted for a week; then, at last, every trace of snow disappeared from the roofs, and Aristide mended the gutters.

A restlessness awoke in us as winter drew to its end. Perhaps someone would come to find us: perhaps something would finally happen. Our exile had to have an end too. The roads which separated us from the world seemed shorter; the post arrived more often. All our chilblains gradually got better.

There is a kind of uniform monotony in the fate of man. Our lives unfold according to ancient, unchangeable laws, according to an invariable and ancient rhythm. Our dreams are never realized and as soon as we see them betrayed we realize that the most intense joys of our life have nothing to do with reality. No sooner do we see them betrayed than we are consumed with regret for the time when they glowed within us. And in this succession of hopes and regrets our life slips by.

My husband died in Rome, in the prison of Regina Coeli, a few months after we left the Abruzzi. Faced with the horror of his solitary death, and faced with the anguish that preceded his death, I ask myself if this happened to us—to us, who bought oranges at Giro's and went for walks in the snow. At that time I believed in a simple and happy future, rich with hopes that were fulfilled, with experiences and plans that were shared. But that was the best time of my life, and only now that it has gone from me forever—only now do I realize it.

1944

GIOVANNI BOCCACCIO (1313–1375) was the son of a Florentine merchant and spent his formative years in Naples. He was an important humanist who lived through the Black Death and described its ravages with timeless empathy, irony and humor in *The Decameron*. His narrative fiction inspired Chaucer, Shakespeare and Tennyson.

CAMILLO BOITO (1836–1914) was a novelist, architect, art historian and engineer. He wrote several collections of short stories.

ANDREA DE CARLO (1952–) is a popular contemporary Italian author who grew up in Milan and has written some twenty novels.

GRAZIA DELEDDA (1871–1936) was a Sardinian-born novelist and winner of the 1926 Nobel Prize for Literature.

NATALIA GINZBURG (1916–1991) was born in Palermo but her family soon moved to Turin; she later memorialized her childhood in her autobiographical work *Family Lexicon*. This book was awarded the Strega Prize, Italy's most prominent literary award, in 1963. She was a political activist, translated Proust and Flaubert into Italian, and served in the Italian parliament.

ANNA MARIA ORTESE (1914–1998) is one of the most celebrated and original Italian writers of the last century. Her book of short stories and reportage, *Neapolitan Chronicles*, brought her widespread acclaim in her native country when it was first published in 1953 and won the prestigious Premio Viareggio.

LUIGI PIRANDELLO (1867–1936) was a dramatist, short story writer and novelist. He won the Nobel Prize for Literature in 1934.

MATILDE SERAO (1856–1927) lived most of her life in Naples. She was among the first professional women writers in modern Italy. Author of many novels, short stories, and essays, she co-founded Naples' leading daily newspaper (*Il Mattino*) and was friends with Edith Wharton and Henry James, who wrote about her work.

GIOVANNI VERGA (1840–1922) was a Sicilian author of novels and short stories whose tale *Cavalleria Rusticana* became the basis for a play and a famed opera.

"White Dogs in the Snow"
From the novel *Tecniche di seduzione*
translated by LeeAnn Geiberger Bortolussi

"Winter in the Abruzzi"
translated by Dick Davis

"Christmas Eve"
translated by Christine Donougher

"Family Interior"
translated by Ann Goldstein and Jenny McPhee

"Black Bread"
translated by D. H. Lawrence

"The Fifth Story
Day the Seventh"
From *The Decameron* by Giovanni Boccaccio
translated by John Payne

"Canituccia"
"To the Tenth Muse"
translated by Jon R. Snyder

"A Dream of Christmas"
"The Golden Cross"
translated by Adrian Nathan West

A VERY FRENCH CHRISTMAS

A continuation of the very popular Very Christmas Series, this collection brings together the best French Christmas stories of all time in an elegant and vibrant collection featuring classics by Guy de Maupassant and Alphonse Daudet, plus stories by the esteemed twentieth century author Irène Némirovsky and contemporary writers Dominique Fabre and Jean-Philippe Blondel. With a holiday spirit conveyed through sparkling Paris streets, opulent feasts, wandering orphans, flickering desire, and more than a little wine, this collection proves that the French have mastered Christmas.

A VERY RUSSIAN CHRISTMAS

This is Russian Christmas celebrated in supreme pleasure and pain by the greatest of writers, from Dostoevsky and Tolstoy to Chekhov and Teffi. The dozen stories in this collection will satisfy every reader, and with their wit, humor, and tenderness, packed full of sentimental songs, footmen, whirling winds, solitary nights, snow drifts, and hopeful children, the collection proves that Nobody Does Christmas Like the Russians.

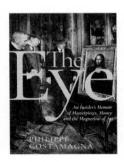

THE EYE
BY PHILIPPE COSTAMAGNA

It's a rare and secret profession, comprising a few dozen people around the world equipped with a mysterious mixture of knowledge and innate sensibility. Summoned to Swiss bank vaults, Fifth Avenue apartments, and Tokyo storerooms, they are entrusted by collectors, dealers, and museums to decide if a coveted picture is real or fake and to determine if it was painted by Leonardo da Vinci or Raphael. *The Eye* lifts the veil on the rarified world of connoisseurs devoted to the authentication and discovery of Old Master artworks.

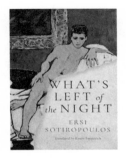

WHAT'S LEFT OF THE NIGHT
BY ERSI SOTIROPOULOS

Constantine Cavafy arrives in Paris in 1897 on a trip that will deeply shape his future and push him toward his poetic inclination. With this lyrical novel, tinged with an hallucinatory eroticism that unfolds over three unforgettable days, celebrated Greek author Ersi Sotiropoulos depicts Cavafy in the midst of a journey of self-discovery across a continent on the brink of massive change. A stunning portrait of a budding author—before he became C.P. Cavafy, one of the 20th century's greatest poets—that illuminates the complex relationship of art, life, and the erotic desires that trigger creativity.

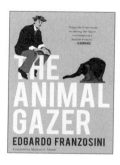

THE ANIMAL GAZER
BY EDGARDO FRANZOSINI

A hypnotic novel inspired by the strange and fascinating life of sculptor Rembrandt Bugatti, brother of the fabled automaker. Bugatti obsessively observes and sculpts the baboons, giraffes, and panthers in European zoos, finding empathy with their plight and identifying with their life in captivity. Rembrandt Bugatti's work, now being rediscovered, is displayed in major art museums around the world and routinely fetches large sums at auction. Edgardo Franzosini recreates the young artist's life with intense lyricism, passion, and sensitivity.

ALLMEN AND THE DRAGONFLIES
BY MARTIN SUTER

Johann Friedrich von Allmen has exhausted his family fortune by living in Old World grandeur despite present-day financial constraints. Forced to downscale, Allmen inhabits the garden house of his former Zurich estate, attended by his Guatemalan butler, Carlos. This is the first of a series of humorous, fast-paced detective novels devoted to a memorable gentleman thief. A thrilling art heist escapade infused with European high culture and luxury that doesn't shy away from the darker side of human nature.

THE MADELEINE PROJECT
BY CLARA BEAUDOUX

A young woman moves into a Paris apartment and discovers a storage room filled with the belongings of the previous owner, a certain Madeleine who died in her late nineties, and whose treasured possessions nobody seems to want. In an audacious act of journalism driven by personal curiosity and humane tenderness, Clara Beaudoux embarks on *The Madeleine Project*, documenting what she finds on Twitter with text and photographs, introducing the world to an unsung 20th century figure.

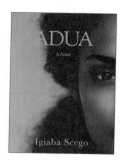

ADUA
BY IGIABA SCEGO

Adua, an immigrant from Somalia to Italy, has lived in Rome for nearly forty years. She came seeking freedom from a strict father and an oppressive regime, but her dreams of film stardom ended in shame. Now that the civil war in Somalia is over, her homeland calls her. She must decide whether to return and reclaim her inheritance, but also how to take charge of her own story and build a future.

If Venice Dies
by Salvatore Settis

Internationally renowned art historian Salvatore Settis ignites a new debate about the Pearl of the Adriatic and cultural patrimony at large. In this fiery blend of history and cultural analysis, Settis argues that "hit-and-run" visitors are turning Venice and other landmark urban settings into shopping malls and theme parks. This is a passionate plea to secure the soul of Venice, written with consummate authority, wide-ranging erudition and élan.

The Madonna of Notre Dame
by Alexis Ragougneau

Fifty thousand people jam into Notre Dame Cathedral to celebrate the Feast of the Assumption. The next morning, a beautiful young woman clothed in white kneels at prayer in a cathedral side chapel. But when someone accidentally bumps against her, her body collapses. She has been murdered. This thrilling novel illuminates shadowy corners of the world's most famous cathedral, shedding light on good and evil with suspense, compassion and wry humor.

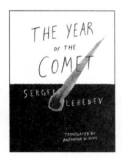

The Year of the Comet
by Sergei Lebedev

A story of a Russian boyhood and coming of age as the Soviet Union is on the brink of collapse. Lebedev depicts a vast empire coming apart at the seams, transforming a very public moment into something tender and personal, and writes with stunning beauty and shattering insight about childhood and the growing consciousness of a boy in the world.

The Last Weynfeldt
by Martin Suter

Adrian Weynfeldt is an art expert in an international auction house, a bachelor in his mid-fifties living in a grand Zurich apartment filled with costly paintings and antiques. Always correct and well-mannered, he's given up on love until one night—entirely out of character for him—Weynfeldt decides to take home a ravishing but unaccountable young woman and gets embroiled in an art forgery scheme that threatens his buttoned up existence. This refined page-turner moves behind elegant bourgeois facades into darker recesses of the heart.

MOVING THE PALACE
BY CHARIF MAJDALANI

A young Lebanese adventurer explores the wilds of Africa, encountering an eccentric English colonel in Sudan and enlisting in his service. In this lush chronicle of far-flung adventure, the military recruit crosses paths with a compatriot who has dismantled a sumptuous palace and is transporting it across the continent on a camel caravan. This is a captivating modern-day Odyssey in the tradition of Bruce Chatwin and Paul Theroux.

THE 6:41 TO PARIS
BY JEAN-PHILIPPE BLONDEL

Cécile, a stylish 47-year-old, has spent the weekend visiting her parents outside Paris. By Monday morning, she's exhausted. These trips back home are stressful and she settles into a train compartment with an empty seat beside her. But it's soon occupied by a man she recognizes as Philippe Leduc, with whom she had a passionate affair that ended in her brutal humiliation 30 years ago. In the fraught hour and a half that ensues, Cécile and Philippe hurtle towards the French capital in a psychological thriller about the pain and promise of past romance.

ON THE RUN WITH MARY
BY JONATHAN BARROW

Shining moments of tender beauty punctuate this story of a youth on the run after escaping from an elite English boarding school. At London's Euston Station, the narrator meets a talking dachshund named Mary and together they're off on escapades through posh Mayfair streets and jaunts in a Rolls-Royce. But the youth soon realizes that the seemingly sweet dog is a handful; an alcoholic, nymphomaniac, drug-addicted mess who can't stay out of pubs or off the dance floor. *On the Run with Mary* mirrors the horrors and the joys of the terrible 20th century.

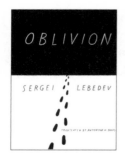

OBLIVION
BY SERGEI LEBEDEV

In one of the first 21st century Russian novels to probe the legacy of the Soviet prison camp system, a young man travels to the vast wastelands of the Far North to uncover the truth about a shadowy neighbor who saved his life, and whom he knows only as Grandfather II. Emerging from today's Russia, where the ills of the past are being forcefully erased from public memory, this masterful novel represents an epic literary attempt to rescue history from the brink of oblivion.

THE LAST SUPPER
BY KLAUS WIVEL

Alarmed by the oppression of 7.5 million Christians in the Middle East, journalist Klaus Wivel traveled to Iraq, Lebanon, Egypt, and the Palestinian territories to learn about their fate. He found a minority under threat of death and humiliation, desperate in the face of rising Islamic extremism and without hope their situation will improve. An unsettling account of a severely beleaguered religious group living, so it seems, on borrowed time. Wivel asks, Why have we not done more to protect these people?

GUYS LIKE ME
BY DOMINIQUE FABRE

Dominique Fabre, born in Paris and a life-long resident of the city, exposes the shadowy, anonymous lives of many who inhabit the French capital. In this quiet, subdued tale, a middle-aged office worker, divorced and alienated from his only son, meets up with two childhood friends who are similarly adrift. He's looking for a second act to his mournful life, seeking the harbor of love and a true connection with his son. Set in palpably real Paris streets that feel miles away from the City of Light, a stirring novel of regret and absence, yet not without a glimmer of hope.

ANIMAL INTERNET
BY ALEXANDER PSCHERA

Some 50,000 creatures around the globe—including whales, leopards, flamingoes, bats and snails—are being equipped with digital tracking devices. The data gathered and studied by major scientific institutes about their behavior will warn us about tsunamis, earthquakes and volcanic eruptions, but also radically transform our relationship to the natural world. Contrary to pessimistic fears, author Alexander Pschera sees the Internet as creating a historic opportunity for a new dialogue between man and nature.

KILLING AUNTIE
BY ANDRZEJ BURSA

A young university student named Jurek, with no particular ambitions or talents, finds himself with nothing to do. After his doting aunt asks the young man to perform a small chore, he decides to kill her for no good reason other than, perhaps, boredom. This short comedic masterpiece combines elements of Dostoevsky, Sartre, Kafka, and Heller, coming together to produce an unforgettable tale of murder and—just maybe—redemption.

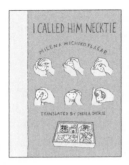

I CALLED HIM NECKTIE
BY MILENA MICHIKO FLAŠAR

Twenty-year-old Taguchi Hiro has spent the last two years of his life living as a hikikomori—a shut-in who never leaves his room and has no human interaction—in his parents' home in Tokyo. As Hiro tentatively decides to reenter the world, he spends his days observing life from a park bench. Gradually he makes friends with Ohara Tetsu, a salaryman who has lost his job. The two discover in their sadness a common bond. This beautiful novel is moving, unforgettable, and full of surprises.

WHO IS MARTHA?
BY MARJANA GAPONENKO

In this rollicking novel, 96-year-old ornithologist Luka Levadski foregoes treatment for lung cancer and moves from Ukraine to Vienna to make a grand exit in a luxury suite at the Hotel Imperial. He reflects on his past while indulging in Viennese cakes and savoring music in a gilded concert hall. Levadski was born in 1914, the same year that Martha—the last of the now-extinct passenger pigeons—died. Levadski himself has an acute sense of being the last of a species. This gloriously written tale mixes piquant wit with lofty musings about life, friendship, aging and death.

New Vessel Press

To purchase these titles and for more information please visit newvesselpress.com.